The Books of Leiden

All Light and Darkness

Volume 1

Written by

A. Henrie Gillett

S&P Books

For Felipe,

*You said you would
read a book if I wrote it.
Well, here you go.*

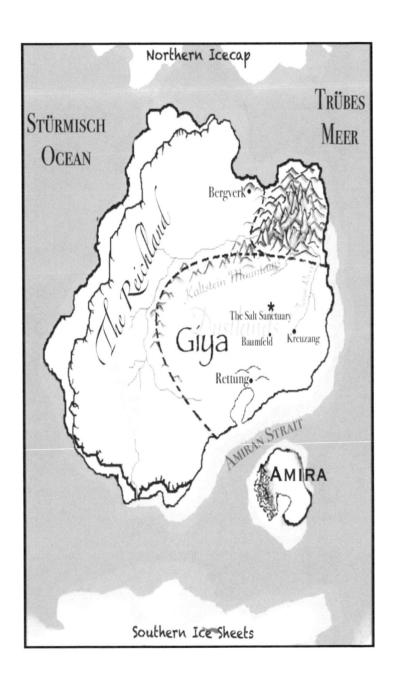

Table of Contents

The heart is in the eyes.
A devil is a person who lives
with their eyes closed.

Prologue

Sagrim slid in the gravel and dust, moving carefully but quickly down the spiralling ramp, one foot forward and the other back and a hand to glide along the centre pillar for balance. The path had steps, but the steps were less steps and more rough-hewn grooves in the stone, typical architecture for the Underworld. There were never steps, only ancient dilapidated lifts and these grooved ramps.

Her decent slowed and gradually levelled as she reached the bottom of the spiral. She exited the ramp tower onto a ledge where all sides were sheer drops into a large room. The drop was only a few meters, but there was no way down. She imagined that, once upon a time, a lift has carried passengers and cargo up and down these sheer drops. Now, though, there was nothing but cracked and crumbling walls of stone. Even the ceiling above her head was suspect. Occasionally, pebbles and dust would break away and sprinkle down.

But there was electricity, bulbs set in lantern-like casings that hung from the ceiling, their light brightly white and unflickering.

How Jesebel had managed that, Sagrim didn't know. Perhaps she piggybacked on electricity from the modern buildings above the Underworld? Perhaps they were always here. The Underworld was a strange place with much unheard of technology. Archaeologists and re-engineers would kill to get their hands on it.

That's why Jesebel rarely allowed people in. As far Sagrim knew, only she and Trip were allowed to see how to get in and out, but even they weren't allowed to wander it freely. This was Jesebel's world, and she guarded it and its secrets fiercely.

Ahead of Sagrim, Jesebel sat on one of the crumbling ledges with her pipe clenched in her teeth. The seemingly old woman had her springy grey hair pulled back and hidden beneath a flat cap, and she wore her typical odd assortment of clothes—a sweater beneath coveralls and an oversized, nappy fur coat over that, and two hideous scarves made from patchworks of rags. She looked homeless, to be sure, but she dressed like this all of the time. For reasons beyond Sagrim's comprehension, she enjoyed the clash of colours and textures, but it was never Sagrim's job to comprehend her boss.

Sagrim cleared her throat. "The banquet is about to begin. We're right on schedule. I'll dress now and follow this group up."

Jesebel pulled away her pipe from her wrinkled lips and let out a curling ribbon of smoke from her mouth. The smell of the strauch bark was pungent and sweet, reminding Sagrim of the funeral incense the strauch trees were also used for.

"Sit," Jesebel said, her voice deep and course. "Talk with me a bit."

Sagrim sat beside her boss, allowing her legs to dangle off the ledge, but held her posture severely straight. In the room below them, three people changed their clothes into animal costumes. It's how they'd arranged to get into the banquet hall undetected, as acrobats.

Bits of fur and feathers from their costumes littered the floor, and several trunks where the customized costumes had been stored crowded it further along with mirror vanities cluttered with makeup and paints. The rest of the floor space had beige canvas bags—the kind tents were usually stored in—scattered here and there, most of them empty now. These had held guns and knives, spears and swords, all the weapons that were now hidden in two dozen acrobat costumes.

Two men were dressed in the yellow and brown spots of a giraffe and practiced walking on stilts. Giraffes, zebras, cranes, and elephants—those mythical creatures were the theme for tonight's operation.

"Remember, Syn," Jesebel yells at one of the men, a smile in her craggy voice, "you're the ass, so don't fall on your arse!"

The other two people changing laughed

uproariously, more enthusiastic than need be. It was their nerves, strung tight with anxiety. That's why Jesebel cracked the joke. She knew her people were on edge. Not that Sagrim could blame them. There were supposed to be Devils there tonight. Several, in fact.

Hard to laugh when you're about to face the best killers on the continent, even if it's only to create a diversion, not to win against them.

The one named Syn hopped down from his stilts. Then he took one of the stilts and pulled it into two pieces. From inside, he retrieved a double-headed spear. He checked the two spearheads, touching their points, nodded in satisfaction, and returned the spear to the interior of the stilt. The other two performing costume changes made similar preparations. The other man carried a hand canon in the puppetry of his giraffe head. The last person, a woman dressed like a cat, double-checked rows of throwing knives neatly stored beneath her zip-on fur.

This was the last group that needed to change into their acrobat disguises. Sagrim had led them here in small groups from the waiting room beneath the banquet hall. She took them through hidden hallways and secret tunnels to reach this room in the Underworld. Jesebel had required them to be blindfolded the entire way so they couldn't find their way back into the Underworld. Once they dressed and armed themselves, Sagrim had led them back to the waiting room and collected the next group. That way their employers never noticed anyone missing.

Not that their employers noticed them much at all. Everyone on this operation was a low-ranked Lowly with obvious inhuman traits like colourful pigments in their skin or physical features like claws or horns. Sagrim herself had vibrant fuchsia coloured eyes and keratinized spines that grew from the centre of her skull and down her back. Supposedly it gave their troop the affectation of fascinating hideousness. At the same time, it kept security from watching them too closely.

"What did our contact have to say?" Jesebel asked, returning her pipe to her mouth.

"Someone matching Muenchen's description arrived

in Bergverk a few days ago. The creature didn't stay though. Apparently, it left again after a few hours and headed for the Dustlands."

Jesebel frowned, the wrinkles creasing her face deeply. "So, someone here told her where to find her corpse. That's troubling."

Sagrim accepted the strange words in stride. She had been with Jesebel since she was little, such strangeness was par for the course with Jesebel. If Jesebel wanted to call a walking calamity "her," so be it. If she wanted to call its ancient ruins a "corpse," Sagrim would accept that, too.

"Should we pursue it?" Sagrim asked.

"Oh, I'm sure we will, but one thing at a time. What about the queen? Does that lab have one?"

Sagrim nodded in acknowledgement. "She said there was a queen insect present, but the Neo-Arkists moved it a week ago. Only drones are left."

"And Wilhelm?"

"He understands the situation and accepts the risks. He'll cooperate with the extraction along with our contact. Fortunately, his children are already in hiding. They'll meet him in Rettung."

"Our people know they're coming?"

"Yes."

"We can't let them fall into the wrong hands—for our sakes as well as theirs."

"Understood."

Jesebel removed her pipe, allowing the smoke to escape with a sigh. "Trouble… Whoever is meddling in Bergverk is set on making trouble, and I suspect it may be someone I know."

She puffed on the pipe silently, a small train engine with plumes of smoke trailing from either corner of her mouth. "Eight hundred years…" she muttered. "I suppose it's time for me to reap what I've sewn."

Sagrim listened quietly. Jesebel excelled in meddling and trouble, so for her to be concerned this time… The impending operation hardly worried Sagrim; yet, at Jesebel's words, the first stirrings of unease settled in her chest.

"Time for you to get ready," Jesebel mumbled, pipe

clenched between her teeth.

Sagrim nodded and leapt from the ledge, landing in a crouch at the bottom. The three people already at the bottom stared at her in shock, but it only lasted a moment. It wasn't the first time they'd seen such feats from her.

"Once I'm done, we'll go back up to the waiting room," Sagrim informed them. "It is about time for us to take the stage."

They nodded in response, expressions tense and serious. Then they busied themselves with the last of their preparations.

Sagrim opened her trunk and retrieved a costume of white feathers. She'd strap her mag-guns to the inside of the wings. It'd be heavy, but no matter, she wouldn't need to keep up the acrobat façade for long.

Part 1

Bergverk City of the Reichland,
the last stronghold of the Guild Coalition Government

Chapter 1: Serpents and BellyDraggers

'Six Devils sit at a high table in a hall met for peace.' It sounds like the beginning of a fairy tale...

Except I am one of those Devils, and this is not a fairy tale.

We sit at the high table arranged for Vogt Faction delegates—not that anyone knows we're Devils. For us to be able to waltz into this banquet undetected, someone high-up in the Coalition Government must have betrayed them.

I don't think we've ever had an operation with so many Devils in one place before, and we all have targets we've been assigned to eliminate: the leader of a major religion and his supporters, the heads of the Coalition Government's ministries, and the heirs of their patron Great Houses… Instead of a Peace Banquet for negotiating a truce, tonight will be a bloodbath that ends the war.

Then there's the secret laboratory Perri has been hunting down and the traitor that runs it. They will be the justification, the reason. There always has to be a reason.

I examine the room, noting the layout, the faces, any potential weapons and where they'd be hidden, but also allowing my koganzug auxiliary to scan the room for more subtle details through my own eyes.

The table we sit at is made from a single slab of pink-veined saltstone, and it spans several meters. The pink saltstone comes from my home country, Giya. It must have cost a fortune to ship over the mountains. The porcelain plates with gold filigree must cost just as much. Silver utensils. Crystal decanters. Wine and strauch bark cigars. Chandeliers lit by electricity hang from a vaulted ceiling above a combat arena in the centre of the room.

The combat arena is the focal point. It is a tidy circle

dropped into the floor by about two meters. White sand covers its floor, but a subtle line in the sand down the middle implies the seam of a trapdoor mechanism.

'Thirteen, what is the trapdoor for?' I ask, speaking silently to my koganzug auxiliary, Koganzug Auxiliary 013, using subvocalization. Thirteen reads my words through the muscles of my lips, mouth, and throat.

It is traditionally used for the entrance of combatants and performers into the arena, he replies, his words transferred directly to my cochlear nerve. *However, it is connected to Bergverk's sewer system so it can also be used to flood the arena with water.*

His voice is neutral, not too high for a man nor too low for a woman. I'm the one that chooses masculine pronouns for him. When he asked why, I told him it was my choice since he was in my head.

'Why flood it?' I ask.

For water battles and performances, of course, but there is another more functional use. Take a guess!

I wait for him to continue, but he doesn't. Thirteen always volunteers the information I don't want and forces me to demand the information I do.

"Thirteen," I growl warningly.

Fine.

Rinsing off the blood. Some of the games they play here drench the sand in blood. They have to clean it somehow. Flooding it works well. I even found a source that says some fighters will literally bathe in the blood of their enemies after a tournament.

You humans, fastidiously clean one moment and so unsanitary at another.

I ignore his observations. Humans make about as much sense to him as lawns in the desert. Not that I understand people much better, but I'd never admit as much to him.

'Keep scanning,' I subvocalize and continue scanning the chamber.

Circular tables occupy the floor and surround the arena like planets orbiting a star. Politicians, officers, merchants, and Immaculates mingle at those tables, some sitting and some standing. Lowlies dressed in tidy suits wait on the tables, weaving between them with trays of drinks and cigars.

From my vantage, I can clearly watch three-hundred people pretend they haven't been at war with each other for two decades, longer than I've been alive.

The arrival of a familiar figure diverts my attention. A woman of medium build wearing a gauzy green dress and curly pink hair approaches our table and leans toward me. A curl of hair falls into her face and she gracelessly blows it away.

"My dear Tantan," she teases, "you look quite the handsome lad this evening. That uniform suits you."

Even though she's one of my fellow Devils, I maintain a stony expression and nod curtly. "Delegate."

Tonight, we Devils play the role of delegates from the Vogt Faction here to negotiate a truce with the Coalition Government. It would finally conclude a war that began before I was born.

Two decades ago, the Coalition Government's department responsible for internal security and pacification, the Vogt der Wahrheit, rebelled and ignited the Reichland's ongoing civil war.

Serpents and BellyDraggers

In reality, this is only the beginning. The Vogt Faction has no intention of stopping with the Reichland. We Devils are from the Vogt, but we are not here for peace. Just to end the war.

I tug at the high collar chafing my neck, watching guests as they enter and sit. Considering the fancy duds and bobbles, these people look like they dressed for a club rather than a war council. Not that I'm dressed much different.

I wear an officer's uniform, a pretentious jacket-slacks-hat ensemble completed by shiny medals on the breast pockets and a fur-collared cape. Only two bits on me are of my own choosing: the plague blade cinched to my ribs beneath the jacket and a red scarf, called a schal, wrapped around my neck.

I've had the schal with me since before Bann brought me to the Vogt. I'm not sure where I got it from, but I'm not comfortable anywhere without it. The Captain wrapped and tucked it for tonight so I'd be wearing it like a dandy.

I feel like a damn peacock, but Captain Bann said

since I insist on wearing a pretty face, I have to wear a pretty uniform to match.

My koganzug combat armour is set to imitate my true flesh so the biomechs that cover me from head to toe portray falsely soft bronze-coloured armour similar to my own skin, and the facial armour replicates my features underneath it. But only I know this mask portrays my true face. Even the other Devils don't know what I actually look like, and I don't know their true faces either.

Sometimes I wonder if I wear my true face to remind me of who I am, or if it is to trick myself into believing there is no devil hidden beneath the mask.

"Not like I chose this face," I grumble quietly as Agent Perchta, the woman in the green dress, slips into the seat beside me.

Agent Perchta grimaces. "'Delegate'? Come now, Tantan. It's 'Perri.' Call me 'Perri,' damn it."

I nod again. "Delegate."

She groans dramatically and leans back in her chair. "Seven years and you haven't once called me 'Perri.'

Can't you say it tonight? Please..."

I raise an eyebrow—a clear 'no' for me.

In response, she acts like a child throwing a fit, huffing and whining.

This is how we are, Perri and me. She is 'Agent Perchta' on my tongue but 'Perri' in my mind. She calls me 'Tantan,' short for Agent Leviatan, with her mouth but 'brother' with her heart.

Perri leans forward, putting her face close to mine, and smirks. "A domestic urvogel."

"What?" I answer, confused.

"Last month, Thirteen asked you what animal you would be to match your personality. I heard you muttering about it. You'd be a domestic urvogel—a kept animal that will bite even the people it likes. All attitude and anger."

Oh! I like that, Thirteen responds excitedly.

Then, absently, Perri adds, "Never meant to be caged but too afraid to fly."

What does she mean by that? Thirteen asks.

Perri's expression is far away.

'She's not talking about me,' I subvocalize to Thirteen.

A domestic urvogel… But if the criteria met is merely your bad attitude, why not a bellydragger or a spined rat? Then there are compsos and…

I groan and force Thirteen's rambling to the back of my mind. Perchta brought up the question just to get Thirteen talking. Once he starts it'll be a long time before he shuts up. The fool AI only behaves himself if Kog Prime, the Kognitive Primary that all the auxiliaries are auxiliary to, syncs to listen in on us.

Perri's thoughts return to the here and now, and her vibrant eyes glitter with mischief. "I knew that would work."

"Damn survey questions," I grumble. "What's the point? He doesn't understand a lick of my answers."

Perri leans back again, a satisfied smirk on her face. "A 'lick'? Watch it Tantan, your backwater roots are showing."

"Backwater?" I ask. "I grew up in the Dustlands. What water?"

Perri cocks her head thoughtfully. "Why is it you can't remember your childhood but you know you're from the Dustlands?"

"Captain Bann told me."

She frowns, picking at her fork. "And you trust everything he tells you?"

I shrug. "He saved my life."

"That doesn't mean you owe him a lifetime," she replies sharply.

I study Perri's expression. It looks distant again.

Technically, Perri and I don't know each other that well—only as well as two people who don't know each other's names or faces—but I'm closer to her than anyone else.

I was dying when I arrived at the Vogt. Bann got me the installation surgery to fix me up, but then I nearly died during recovery. It was Perri who took care of me and kept me alive. Then we apprenticed together under Captain Bann for two years, even earned our Devil's masks around the same time. We've been Devils for five years—she chose to specialise in espionage while I stayed at Captain Bann's side.

No, I don't know her well, but after seven years together, I know her well enough to see she has something on her mind tonight.

Guests arrive in greater numbers and proceed into the banquet hall, suggesting the Peace Banquet will soon begin.

I let Perri alone and turn my attention back to the banquet. Once or twice, my biomechs stir restlessly, experiencing a surge caused by interference from another koganzug user being near me, but unless they're here for my plague blade or Devil's mask, we're of no concern to one another. Kog Prime has us all well in hand regardless of whose side we think we're on. Instead, I note the little symbols of status in the crowd, knowing Thirteen will be noting them, too.

The watches, pens, cufflinks, rings, and pendants— some of them heirloom relics and some of them high-end reengineered copies—signify wealth. Embroidery on backs of jackets and breast pockets and pins on lapels display Great House affiliations. All symbols of wealth, connections, and professions.

But ultimately, none of these things can compare to the status that comes with the bodies they were born with—blood status.

The most powerful people in the room look entirely human and were born looking that way: hair and eyes in distinctly human shades of browns, blues, and the occasional green; skin in distinctly human tones without streaks or blotches; no claws, horns, pointed teeth, or slotted pupils; and, no surgeries to make them appear that way. As divine as the Twelve Noahs when they fell from the Lights Above. Born without stain or flaw. Immaculately human.

The Immaculates and the Great House bloodlines— they are the most powerful people in the room.

The civil war between the Vogt Faction and incumbent Coalition Government has lasted two decades, but the war for dominance among the Immaculate Great Houses has lasted centuries.

Even now, that ancient war rages. Five true Immaculates socialise on the main floor: four standing or sitting around the circular tables and one sitting at the Coalition high table. Two of them will die tonight. Perhaps I will be the one to kill them.

'Thirteen, has our target arrived?' I subvocalize to Thirteen, mouth moving without voicing the words.

...but the biggest reason I thought you'd say 'moose' is because...

Lights Above, he's still talking about the survey question. I close my eyes and take a deep breath.

"Thirteen," I warn, vocalizing out of irritation.

Our target, the current Noah of the Arkist Church, is in attendance, he answers quickly.

He sounds too formal, his voice too regulated and monotone. Kog Prime must be listening in on us since that's the only times when Thirteen behaves.

Each auxiliary acts as a host for its koganzug user, allowing the central Kognitive Primary system to connect to them through the Kognitive Network. An auxiliary also manipulates the biomechs that make up a koganzug user's combat armour and manages the intel downloaded to a user's kog port. It also monitors and reports its user's behaviour to Kog Prime.

The koganzug tech implanted during my installation surgery, hardware that is now interwoven throughout my body, mimics the functions of my anatomy, becoming a secondary system for my senses that Thirteen can access and manipulate. But, while my body needs rest, Thirteen's systems run on the power stored in my koganzug so Thirteen can monitor my surroundings even while I sleep. It also means that Kog Prime can watch everything I do unless I have the permissions for dark mode, which will disconnect me from the Kognitive Network. Even then, once Thirteen syncs with Kog Prime again, it will know everything I did during its absence.

It makes the relationship between koganzug user and auxiliary both intimate and awkward. It doesn't help that my auxiliary is particularly odd.

'Thirteen, show me the target's location.'

Thirteen pauses. When he speaks again, his pretentious robotic voice is gone; Kog Prime no longer listening. *Not hard to spot him,* he says. *It's an old man that looks like he passed gas and doesn't want anyone to know.*

'Thirteen,' I warn again. 'Show me.'

Two o'clock. Two hundred meters.

I look where Thirteen indicated, and Thirteen clarifies my eyesight. I study the face of the grizzled old man I'm supposed to kill tonight. His stern expression is tight with anxiety. He looks as if he'd rather not be here. Maybe he senses what's about to happen?

I dread the confrontation. Best if he never sees me coming. The fear of death and the pain that comes before are both far worse than death itself.

Why are we going to kill the Noah? Thirteen asks, sounding confused. *I thought the Arkists are on our side now.*

'Only some are,' I answer, studying a middle-aged woman in a suit standing to his left.

Her suit is military style, double row of buttons and a high, stiff collar, but she's not military. Her hair is thick and black and cut blunt at the jaw. Bangs make a straight edge across her forehead. Everything is stiff and hard lines with her. She plays the part of an Immaculate well, but she can't hide the scars from me. I'd bet my life she had her ears trimmed.

What is the difference? Thirteen asks.

'We're supposed to kill the Noah. Doesn't that answer your questions?'

No.

'Identify the woman to the left of the target.'

Clara Neuseman. What about her?

'Manny brought her in to visit the Commander a few months back. Why would he do that?'

She proposed and negotiated the alliance between the Arkist Church and the Vogt Faction and is the figurehead of the popular Neo-Arkist Movement within the Arkist Church.

'That started the hollowbern cleansing?'

Correct. The First Noah commanded humanity to multiply and populate the planet, but hollowberns are cursed to fail this command from birth. Thus, the cleansing.

Hollowberns, the opposite status of Immaculates. Born sterile and marked by the black stains of a blood rot that doesn't kill them.

A lot of people consider them jinxes. Not only do they get blamed if anyone else gets sick—even though it's been proven that blood rot is not contagious—they also get blamed for anything else bad that happens. In fact, the word for 'hollowbern' in Amiran means 'demon.'

"Nothing easier than creating an enemy to solidify a power base, especially if that enemy is already widely hated," I murmur. 'What's the pin on her lapel?'

Thirteen uses its system to zoom my eyesight and focuses the image for me. The pin portrays an old man in a robe holding a giant key. It's the symbol of the Neo-Arkists.

'I get the feeling she'll find a reason to leave early tonight, but she won't take the Noah with her. She'll leave him and his supporters here to die.'

I don't understand.

I wish I didn't.

Serpents and BellyDraggers

The machinations of the human mind never fail to launch Thirteen into loops of confusion. Thirteen wasn't made to grasp the big picture; that's Kog Prime's job. Thirteen and I are merely chess pieces moved by an enigmatic player.

I snort derisively and lean back in my seat, eyesight normalizing. It was people like her who said, let's meet in Bergverk City. Let's make peace. To these people, the prospect of peace is merely bait. Chaos means opportunity while peace means settling.

The Vogt Faction and the Coalition Government; the Immaculate Great Houses and the Lowly slaves; the Arkists and Neo-Arkists, even though they're all here, I doubt there's a grain of sincerity in any of them.

I never would have become a Devil if I'd known it meant serving people like her—if I'd known the Vogt is more mercenary than hero—but I'd had nowhere else to go, and I owed Bann my life. When he found me, I was dying. He brought me back to the Vogt and convinced the Vogt leadership to do the koganzug installation surgery to save my life.

After my apprenticeship, I could have chosen another branch of government to work in or gone to serve a Vogt officer's household, but I thought I could repay him by staying. Bann didn't want me to—said I wasn't cut out to be a Devil—but I thought I could do some good if I stayed by his side. I thought myself loyal. I thought myself a hero.

I thought wrong.

Five years of killing. Five years and the only thing that keeps me going is the thought of walking away someday. Other Devils have resigned, so can I. Then I'll go somewhere no one can find me. Build a little house. Maybe keep some animals. Go fishing... Fishing, not hunting.

But not yet. I still have reasons to stay here. I owe Bann too much, and there's also the fool in green sitting beside me.

Thirteen pipes up again. *Survey question number 3,121...*

I stifle a sigh. Thirteen says my answers to his survey questions will help him to better integrate with me, but the questions are usually complete nonsense…

In your opinion, what are the differences between the metaphorical identities of devils and saints?

…so when he asks nonsense, I answer with nonsense. 'Humans care about only four things: feeling joy, giving joy, feeling pain, and inflicting pain. When humans care about one of these more than the rest, they become devils or saints.'

So, devils and saints are evolutions of humanity?

I snort derisively. 'Yes. So now the world consists of only devils and saints… but mostly devils.'

A horn blares, stifling conversation and turning people's attention to the combat arena. The floor opens and an orchestra appears on a platform that rises through the floor. The music floats over the room, encouraging people to take their seats. The doors leading into the hallways open and waiters stream into the hall carrying trays of food on their shoulders.

Initiate Phase Two, Kog Prime orders, and the Peace Banquet begins.

Chapter 2: Knives in Their Smiles

I refuse to eat the dinner. An urvogel fowl lays untouched on my plate, the plucked wings tied against the body and the snake-like head curled around itself. The chefs left the teeth and claws for show.

I haven't been able to eat urvogel since I was kid. Can't remember why. Can't remember a lot of things.

When I woke from my installation surgery seven years ago, I only knew my name, Leiden Talson. I gave up that name to become the Devil Leviatan, but sometimes I'll see things, or hear them, and feel an impression of something from my past.

A painting of crooked trees set in rows.

An empty house surrounded by sand.

A slamming door.

Knives in Their Smiles

There's a feeling of familiarity, of a thought I can't quite collect, but no clear memories, and I think Kog Prime wants to keep it that way. Whenever I go in for a biomech transfusion or kog port maintenance, my mind seem more scrambled than before, the few pieces of memory I regained becoming vague and foggy once again.

Silver utensils clatter and scrape on the porcelain plates. A man at ten o'clock and two tables over laughs with drunken disregard. The night has only just begun and he's already inebriated.

I massage my temples, easing a sudden headache.

Instead of eating, I take a small block of wood from my pocket, not much bigger than my thumb, and unsheathe my plague blade from my shoulder strap. Wood chips flick into my food and drop to the floor. Even though it's a hard wood, the stone-like blade cuts through it smoothly.

My plague blade looks like something a caveman made—about the length of my forearm with a leather-wrapped hilt and no hilt guard—but though it may look primitive, it has an ingenious locking mechanism that allows one dagger to become two.

Each plague blade is unique, rare, and irreplaceable—an artefact of ancient technology that re-engineers have repeatedly failed to replicate. Some are swords; some are daggers or spears; but, all of them are made from black ore that allows them to pierce koganzug armour, and the wounds they leave quickly become infected with blood rot. They are lethal even to Devils so the 'have nots' regard the 'haves' with murderous envy.

Perri and I have plague blades. Perri has never been willing to tell me how she got hers—something about when she was an express carrier in Giya. I inherited mine from one of the Captain's comrades who resigned. The man decided to leave the Vogt and handed off his mask and plague blade to the Captain to hand down to the next generation of Devils.

Someday, that's what I'll do, too. I'll leave my plague blade and Devil's mask with the Captain and finally be free.

Knives in Their Smiles

My blade works fast on the wood block, chips spraying across the table. A face emerges from the wood—the face of a young man—a young man the Captain killed yesterday because I couldn't. He was little more than a kid—barely old enough for his anger and hatred to spill over—to send him running to the rebels.

The wood grains look like the black stains that streaked the kid's face, the stains of a hollowbern. The stains look too much like the blood rot plague, but he was born with those stains. They would never have killed him, just made it impossible for him to have kids.

Born hollow—hollowbern.

People feared that young man for those stains and scorned him for his infertility. In the Reichland, no hollowbern has a good life… or a long one. Of course he became a rebel. I let a poor kid like that die, and people love me for it—love the Devils like we're some kind of heroes.

People love loving together even if what they love is a monster.

"Making another one, Tantan?" Perri asks, sitting in her chair beside me.

I don't reply. She doesn't expect me to. She knows I think a lot but say little.

Tantan. She's the only one who calls me that. I think she's a few years older than me, already in her twenties. She's set her koganzug armour to replicate clear, pale skin. It's even sprouted false hair for her, springy pink curls that tumble around her head like tufts of pillow stuffing. Her Devil's mask is that of a smirking baboon, but she rarely wears it since she works in espionage. Still, she keeps it—keeps on being a Devil—for the undeniable status it bestows.

We all have our reasons.

She nudges my elbow. "You've got an admirer."

I follow her gaze and discover a young Lowly girl watching me while she slowly clears our plates away. Her hair is pulled back in a braid, displaying tympanic membranes instead of ears. Means she's mostly deaf. She watches my hands, intent on my whittling.

I retrieve a small block of pale, soft wood from

another pocket and start carving it.

What are you making? Thirteen asks. *An animal? I bet it's an animal. You like animals. Is it a bird? No, not a bird. A rodent? Yes, I think it is! Dragon rat? No, why would you make a dragon rat? They're gross. A spined mouse? Horned hamster! Not a hamster...*

With quick, practiced strokes, I carve the block into a rabbit—a mythical immaculate creature from The Annals. She might not be familiar with The Annals, but I think she'll like the long ears and big feet.

A rabbit! I knew it was a rabbit. Wait... Why did you carve a rabbit?

I set the rabbit on my plate, and she skips the Commander and Captain Bann's plates to clear mine. The rabbit disappears, and I allow myself a small smile.

Leviatan! Thirteen yelps. *That child stole your rabbit!*

Sometimes I wonder if entrusting my life to Thirteen is really the best strategy for my survival.

I pick up the figurine I was working on before, but Perri butts into my line of sight so I have to stop whittling. She stares intently at the wooden doll. Not that she needs to. Her auxiliary could have zoomed in so she could get a closer look without moving. She just wants to make me squirm at her proximity. She knows I don't like people close to me, figuratively or literally.

"Are you going to carry this one with you? Do you have enough pockets?"

"No," I answer.

"'No,' you don't have enough pockets?" She smirks.

"No, this is not a totem."

Perri is thinking of the carvings I keep in my locker at headquarters, but those are different than these little figurines. These little figurines… They have everything to do with who I am now. The carvings in my locker are totems, things we Devils keep to help us remember ourselves after Kog Prime meddles with our minds. It happens when there's a software update or sometimes as a punishment if we disobey orders. The totems bring us back to ourselves so all the Devils have a few. Perri keeps hers, a small heirloom music box, with her at all times.

Knives in Their Smiles

In my locker, there are carvings of a toy soldier, an oil lamp, an elephant, a work auto, a necklace pendant of two snakes climbing a winged staff... Then there's the red schal I wear.

These are the things that tell me I'll remember who I was someday. Remember how I became what I am. Maybe even remember how to get back to who I was.

On my right, Manny, short for Agent Mammon, leans past Captain Bann and the Lady Commander to click his tongue at me, taunting me. He grins widely, and even though he's not wearing his hyena mask, the face he wears resembles it. "Heard ya kilt a cur yesterday."

My hand slips, gouging the wood, and Manny laughs.

Cur. Mongrel. A dog with dirty blood. That is what a hollowbern is to Manny. He is a Neo-Arkist and makes no secret of it.

People love to love together; they also love to hate together. Which is worse?

"Did it scream?" Manny asks.

He's asking to taunt me, but I see the hunger in his eyes. He actually wants to know. He savours the bloody details. It's what makes him our head interrogator. Says he prefers 'quality over quantity' when it comes to killing people. In reality, he's just addicted to his endocrine enhancer.

Something dark and ugly turns in my stomach, a beast uncurling. It's a familiar feeling, this Ugly. It has led me through silenced homes and over blood-soaked battlegrounds. It has kept me alive these five years, but it is also what makes me a Devil.

"Did you cut off its useless balls?" Manny hisses with pleasure.

I let the Ugly lead. I move to stand, ready to plunge my plague blade into Manny's hand and pin it to the table, then watch him scream as blood rot eats away his flesh.

Captain Bann grips my shoulder, stopping me from standing, his fingers biting into my armour and muscle. In the same moment, he slams his index finger of his other hand down on the end of a fork, sending it into

Manny's face. Manny swears, tries to stand, but the Lady Commander places a hand on Manny's shoulder and he goes still.

The Captains pulls me back into my seat and leans over to whisper to me. "Put away your blade. I know it looks like something from the midden pile, but it could still give away your identity."

I put away the carving of the hollowbern child and return my plague blade to my shoulder holster. I'm disinclined to draw any more of Manny's attention anyway. He can't take on the Captain so he picks fights with me. If it weren't for the Captain, Manny would have killed me for my plague blade long ago.

Captain Bann looks exceptionally ordinary tonight. He wears a simple, grey military suit with far fewer ribbons and medals than mine and a standard-issue officer's sabre and hand-cannon at his waist. The face he wears is generic in its simplicity. If I didn't know how frightening the Captain could be, it would be funny; instead, it's unnerving. I can't help glancing around for his immense executioner's blade, but of course he must have stowed it somewhere. Too many people would recognise it. It's not a plague blade, but he doesn't need one. He has something more deadly at his disposal.

Aside from Perri, me, and the Captain, three more Devils sit at our high table. The Lady Commander sits beside Captain Bann, then it's the bloodthirsty psycho Manny, and last is Zeb.

The Lady Commander is "the Lady" not because of her gender but because of her status as the heir to the Marcs Great House, one of the oldest Immaculate bloodlines in the world. She's the only Devil whose identity we know all too well, and must always remember.

Zeb, on the other hand, has always been a bit of an enigma. Short for Agent Beelzebub, Zeb acts true to his call-sign tonight. He eats plate after plate of food, turning his space into a mass grave of urvogel bones and food waste. While the rest of us worry our food could be poisoned, as a poison master, he couldn't care less.

Knives in Their Smiles

Thirteen worries about Zeb trying to kill me more than Manny, but he's never shown any inclination despite not having a plague blade. Of course, Thirteen sees that as even more reason to distrust him. Thirteen is being too quiet, I realise. He must have found something to amuse himself. No doubt I'll soon find out. Only deletion could shut Thirteen up and even then, he might still find a way to come back just to ask a stupid question.

What is the purpose of an autograph? Thirteen asks suddenly. *Does it grant the recipient authority in the signers place?*

Speak of the Devil... Here we go.

'No,' I answer. I move my mouth without vocalizing. I could just talk—he hears what I hear and sees what I see—but there are too many people around right now.

Is the signer initiating a contract with the recipient?

'No.'

Does it transfer essence to the recipient, giving him a bond with the signer?

"Gods, no." I can't help speaking aloud this time. "What have you been reading, Thirteen?"

In the theatre production I collected recently, there is something called magic, but it is invoked by emotion. In order to upgrade, the two main characters touch each other's-

"Gods Below," I swear in exasperation. "I wasn't actually asking!"

Perri laughs beside me. She's surprisingly cheerful this evening despite the impending operation. Then again, tonight she's going to be doing data recovery from a secret lab she spent two trips to Bergverk to find. She's never needed two trips to complete a mission before. I'm sure she's excited to finally finish the task tonight.

"Talking about a play?" she asks.

—and after that, one of them touches the other's—

I close my eyes and grit my teeth.

"Did he collect the one about the erotic magic?"

I peer at her. "How do you know?"

She smiles widely. "I've read it too!"

—which is anatomically impossible unless one of them—

"Why isn't Thirteen in your head?" I grumble.

"Because secretly I'm in Thirteen's head," she quips.

I groan and put my forehead to the table.

Perri laughs again. "My auxiliary is warning me to not interfere with others' auxiliaries. She's so rote that I can parrot her." She shakes her head ruefully. "I still can't figure out how Thirteen hasn't been deleted. Kog Prime normally gets rid of deviant auxiliaries within weeks of them showing any personality."

I focus on Perri, moving Thirteen's monologue to the back of my mind, like ignoring a song stuck in my head. Just a song. Not some gods-damned fractured bit of talking hardware implanted into the back of my head.

Perri continues. "Even if he's on his best behaviour when Kog Prime is watching, Kog would still find out everything when it syncs Thirteen's data. Not only that, other auxiliaries' personalities homogenize after syncing, but Thirteen's never seems to." Perri presses her lips together, thoughtful. She places a hand on my shoulder. "I've decided to feel sorry for you, Tantan. Just think of him as a radio you can't turn off."

I shrug off her hand and roll my eyes. "A radio I can't turn off and watches and listens to everything I do and reports it to my superiors."

And saves your life on occasion, Thirteen adds, interrupting himself.

"And nearly gets me killed on others," I retort.

Perri raises an eyebrow. I glower, pointing a thumb at my forehead. Perri snickers in response. Her laughter eases the anxiety writhing in my stomach.

Devils don't trust, but if I could, I'd trust Perri.

The lightbulbs nestled in the chandeliers above our heads dim. The room quiets. People find their seats.

Suddenly, huge flames burst from around the perimeter of the combat arena. All attention turns to the arena. A man in a white tuxedo with a gold bowtie and cummerbund walks across the sand and stands in the middle of the arena floor. From the clothes, he must be part of the Coalition. Vogt people prefer military style clothes even when they're not in uniform.

Knives in Their Smiles

"Welcome! Welcome!" He announces, flourishing his hands and bowing. He speaks Manual, the official language of the Reichland, but it's strongly accented by a local dialect. "We appreciate all in attendance as we gather together to end two decades of conflict between our parties."

I note his choice of words. 'End the conflict,' not 'make peace.'

"We'll now begin our entertainment for the evening. Please welcome the Menagerie of Acrobats. They bring with them something special for the occasion. We know from archaeologists and The Annals of the Twelve Noahs preserved by the Arkist Church"—he nods toward the table where the head of the Arkist Church sits—"that the Twelve Noahs knew strange beasts never before seen on our world. Great lizards larger than houses. Small creatures with fur covering their bodies that fly from tree to tree..."

Costumed acrobats enter the arena as he speaks. They walk on stilts, tumble on the floor, fly in on trapeze, and wear costumes and puppetry reminiscent of the animals the narrator describes. The acrobats must be of lower blood status. Many of them display horns, pointed ears, claws—it seems to add a sort of authenticity to their performance.

"…the largest fish that eat the smallest organisms. Birds that fly through the water…"

The acrobats move gracefully. Their puppetry is both garish and amazing. It's original, something not seen often these days. Most performances are reproductions of excavated ancient classics, or they're demonstrations of newly reengineered technology.

I lean forward in my seat.

This came from someone's imagination. The style and genius reminds me of something… of someone? I can't remember and trying gives me a headache.

"Now, let me present to you…"

The host interrupts my thoughts, draws my attention back to the arena.

"…something never before seen. Let me show for you something mythical and magical and amazing. Something that should not be, but is. Let me show you myth made alive!"

He bows out of the limelight, and behind him, coming out from the trapdoor, is a creature that brings me to my feet. I lean on the table, staring.

An elephant lumbers into the arena, a woman dressed as a white bird crouched on its back. Her ears are pointed and several short, yellow spines protrude along the centre of her shaved scalp; and her eyes are a vibrant fuchsia colour.

The audience applauds politely, and I stare. My head hurts and my vision wavers, but I feel myself moving, passing tables. Passing people. Jumping down.

I find myself standing in the arena, sand beneath my boots, and the elephant a hundred meters away. I look around. People in the audience are on their feet, pointing and whispering: What is he doing? Is this part of the show? What's going on?

Leviatan, report.

It's Kog Prime.

Why are you acting against orders? Please return to your seat.

The elephant continues toward me. Thirteen says something, but it's nothing but a murmur in my mind. The woman dressed as a white bird on top of the elephant smiles at me, her teeth white against her dark skin. There are knives in her smile.

There are knives in all the acrobats' smiles, but I reach out a hand anyway. Palm out. A hand seeking to touch, to know…

A voice shouts from my memories—the voice of a child: "Are elephants real?"

Pain stabs through my head. My body trembles, wanting to collapse, but I continue to reach out.

Maybe… Maybe if I touch the elephant, I'll remember. I'll remember how I became a Devil. Then I'll know how to undo it.

Because somewhere in my past, that past I can't remember, is a small house with a little garden, a few animals, some fishing, and a reason to leave this place.

Chapter 3: A Bad Joke

The elephant charges at me, but I can't move. I don't want to move. I want to know if it is real. I reach toward it.

A sabre, thrown like a spear, stabs into the elephant's neck. It screams, furious. The Captain runs past me, his hand-cannon drawn, and shoots. The ball drills into the elephant's eye, and the elephant stumbles. The bird woman leaps from its back, shouting in another language, and lands behind me. The elephant collapses, spraying sand into my face.

I let my hand drop slowly, stunned, and I stare at the dead elephant.

I should react—the bird woman intends to harm me—but I can't seem to centre myself. I feel trapped in a dream.

The sound of clashing metal drags me out of the dream. Captain Bann has drawn his officer's sword. He battles three acrobats. One with a hand-cannon goes down first, chest bleeding. The other two use spears they disguised as stilts.

Thirteen is yelling at me. *What in shattering hell are you doing? She is going to kill us!*

I turn around as the bird woman rips off her fake wings and retrieves two re-engineered mag-gun revolvers hidden in them. They're a new model, excavated only last year. How'd she get her hands on not one, but two?

Stop gawking and move, if you please. I don't want to die today!

Die? Mag-guns can't pierce koganzug armour—not enough prolonged concentrated force. Swords do more damage than bullets.

She shoots and the mag ball strikes me in the chest, tearing through my uniform.

I'm right, I don't die, but Lights Above, it hurts like

hell.

My koganzug disperses the kinetic energy into its biomechs, but the shot is so close range that my suit can't transfer the energy fast enough. A small explosion erupts around the ball as the nearest biomechs overload and fry, burning my clothes. The unabsorbed energy penetrates the armour, and I feel like I've been kicked in the chest.

The ball returns to her mag-gun, and she shoots again. I move this time, hoping to use my koganzug's enhanced speed to dodge it, but Thirteen actually inhibits my speed, allowing the second mag ball to glance off my shoulder.

"What are you doing?" I hiss, reaching for my plague blade.

No plague blade, Kog Prime orders. You are to maintain your cover as a delegate. Your auxiliary will limit your abilities to be within the range of an anzug user's.

Anzug combat armour—the layman's suit. It provides protection from bullets and enhances strength, but telling a koganzug user to act like they're wearing an anzug is like using a chef's knife for a hatchet. It's doable, but it doesn't feel right.

Hand-to-hand, then.

The bird woman meets me head on. I throw a punch, but she moves faster than I can strike, slipping around me. I might not be able to use all of my speed, but that punch was still fast enough to hit just about anyone.

She smiles at me, knows she caught me off-guard, and sticks her other mag-gun in my belly. Her fuchsia eyes sparkle with glee.

This is going to hurt, Thirteen observes.

Yes… Yes, it is.

I spin to the side so the shot glances off my ribs, but there's a ripping sound and a spray of sparks as biomechs shatter at the impact. The hit takes my breath away.

Bruised ribs, Thirteen reports. My koganzug forms a compress automatically to keep the swelling and pain under control.

"No compress," I shout, dodging one of the mag

balls as it returns to one of the woman's guns. "I need the flexibility."

Thirteen doesn't argue, and the pressure on my chest releases.

I need to get inside her guard so I don't have to keep dancing around those guns.

Thirteen tells me the same.

She shoots again. I make a feint at her, forcing her to fire the other gun. Then I attack, jabbing at her chest before she has time to recall her cannon balls. She realises her mistake and doesn't hesitate to drop her guns. She grabs my wrist. Is she going to try wrestling me? No, she sweeps beneath my strike and tries to throw me, using my momentum against me. I counter, gripping her wrist in return.

We twist and swing, attacking and countering. I've never fought a non-koganzug user who could counter me so well, handicap or no.

I make a hard turn and her grip falters. We're thrown apart. She lands on her feet, skidding in the sand and stopping practically on top of her guns.

A Bad Joke

Damn.

"Damn," Thirteen and I say at the same time.

She grabs her mag-guns and shoots. The ball glances off my armour again as I spin toward her and grab her wrist, pointing the loaded mag-gun at the ceiling as she fires. The ball gets lodged in the crossbeams like I hoped. Then I dance around behind her, bringing her arm up nice and snug between her shoulder blades, her gun still in her hand.

The first ball returns to the mag-gun in her free hand, and she immediately reaches across her body and tucks the barrel into my gut. She doesn't shoot though. Maybe she knows it wouldn't make me let her go, just piss me off.

"Who sent you?" I ask.

She doesn't speak, but her body is shaking.

I... Thirteen hesitates. *I think she's laughing.*

"Tell me," I order, bending her arm farther.

A few meters from us, the Captain takes down a third acrobat. He comes toward us, his officer's sabre retrieved from the elephant's carcass and bloody from combat.

I expect the acrobat fighting me to panic. Instead, she smiles like someone cracked, her fuchsia eyes glittering. Then several balls the size of marbles drop out of the grips of her guns. Smoke erupts from them when they hit the sand. At the same time, she fires the gun pointed at my belly. It lands like a punch to the gut, knocking the breath from me, and she wrenches free.

The other acrobats toss out the small balls as well. The Captain and I withdraw automatically even though Thirteen tells me the smoke isn't toxic. When it clears, the acrobats are gone, including the bodies of their dead. From the tracks in the sand, it looks like they retreated the same way they came, through the trapdoor.

Captain Bann jumps down through the trapdoor but returns soon after.

"They escaped through the sewer," he says. "For them to retreat so smoothly, someone on the inside must have paved the way for them."

So, the Coalition wasn't the only one to get betrayed; there's a spy amongst us as well.

A Bad Joke

The Captain studies the tracks and blood. "Considering their skills, we weren't the only ones going easy. They didn't go after any of the guests; they didn't even try that hard to kill us. What were they after?"

Then the Captain switches his attention to me. He checks me over for injuries then looks me straight in the eye. "What the hell were you thinking?"

My gut clenches. "I…"

I what? I lost my mind? We're Devils—we've all lost our minds, but we never let that interfere with a mission.

The Captain's eyes narrow thoughtfully, but then he shakes his head. "We will talk about this back at headquarters."

I cringe. No doubt Kog Prime will make its presence felt during that conversation.

The Captain goes to interrogate security, leaving me and the dead elephant in the arena. The dead elephant begins to disintegrate. I brush a hand over it, rubbing coarse grains of black dust between my fingers.

It wasn't a real elephant but a golem, a creature made by makerbugs to look and act real. I've never heard of one looking like something from The Annals though. They're usually a mutated form of a native species.

'An engineered golem? Is that even possible?' I subvocalize to Thirteen.

I... don't think so. It's not like makerbugs can read The Annals.

'Then what is this creature and where did these people get it?'

Thirteen doesn't have an answer.

∞

Within a quarter of an hour after the incident, the banquet proceeds as if nothing happened. It's almost like the audience thinks this was all part of the show, or maybe they can't bear to leave the sight of so much Black Dust.

The value of Black Dust is more than gold. The Vogt military uses it in biomech transfusions for koganzug users like me, and supposedly re-engineers can use it to simulate materials they have not successfully re-engineered, yet. The latter sounds like myth to me, though.

Captain Bann speaks with the head of security in the back of the banquet hall. Probably making some excuse as to why he and I are wearing combat armour. Hopefully we kept what kind of armour we use under wraps. Meanwhile, a medic checks me over back at our high table despite my reassurances to the Captain that I'm fine.

I think about Captain Bann's comment—that the fight wasn't their purpose. The attack was poorly orchestrated, to say the least. Then again, I've known people who rushed headlong into more pointless deaths.

The Captain arrests the host who introduced the acrobat troop. He probably won't survive interrogation. I'm sure Manny is salivating with anticipation.

A new host stands in the limelight of the arena and tries to convince the audience that the attack was all part of the show. Lowlies sweep up the remains of the elephant.

The new host tells us the Dust will be gift-wrapped for guests to take home at the end of the night, as if that makes up for the acrobat debacle; and, maybe for these people, a bit of Dust does make up for it. Afterward, the host introduces a group of musicians and the night continues as if nothing happened.

Fools. They ignored their chance to escape. Even the Noah remains in his seat, but Neuseman is no longer at his side.

The medic leaves and I subvocalize to Thirteen. 'What language did the woman on the elephant speak when she jumped from it?'

It takes Thirteen a split second to replay the moment and answer. *A dialect from one of the Islands of Endonia.*

Endonia? She's a long way from home. 'What did she say?'

'*For the Light,*' Thirteen answers. *It is a common war cry used by members of the Children of Light resistance faction.* Thirteen uses a hum again, shorter this time. *It was a clever ploy, like a Trojan horse. Do you think they know that story? But it was an elephant, not a horse. A Trojan elephant? But they're not Trojan-*

I ignore Thirteen's attempt to reinvent history recorded in The Annals. 'Where did they find a golem that looks like an elephant? From what I know of golems, the forms they take are unpredictable.'

Elephants are recounted quite exactly in The Annals, including their anatomy and behaviour. According to the record and what we saw, they match. It seems to have been designed.

A designed golem? What else could they design then? Could they design a person? But I keep my questions to myself. I don't want to delve too deeply. Depth leads to drowning. Then again, so does breadth. Few people realise how hard it is maintain safety in ignorance.

'Maybe they just got lucky,' I reply instead.

The Captain finishes talking and leaves the banquet hall with the head of security.

Right, luck. Luck explains everything... Thirteen trails off before continuing. *Can we go talk to the*

Captain? I want to talk to someone smart.

"Shove off," I swear at him reflexively.

Shove what off?

I ignore Thirteen and glance around the banquet hall, realizing there's someone else missing besides Captain Bann. Perri's seat is empty and I don't see her in the hall.

'Where's Agent Perchta?' I subvocalize.

I don't know. Maybe she stepped out for a smoke?

'Not likely.'

I slip away from the table, nodding to the Lady Commander for permission, and head to the nearest door into the hallway.

Outside of the banquet hall, electric lamps light the hallway, dimmed to present an elegant ambience. The hallway is empty. Aside from those cleaning up the Dust, the other Lowlies have been called away, probably to prepare dessert.

The main hallway circles the banquet hall. Doors entering the banquet hall line the wall every few meters. The far wall displays paintings, ornate light sconces, and grand windows.

I lean against the wall between a sconce and a window, unwrapping my schal so it hangs from my neck, and unbutton the top two buttons of my shirt. I also unfasten the gold chain attaching my cape and let the cape fall to the floor then kick it under the drapes. It's torn from the fight anyway. The shirt under my jacket is torn too, and singed, and I lost my military cap.

I nearly blew our cover. Kog Prime must be pissed… if it can get pissed. I wonder what Captain Bann is saying to get me out of trouble. I joined the Devils thinking I could be of help to the Captain, but it seems like I just make more work for him. No wonder he's turned so cold toward me. He'll probably be relieved once I leave.

I rub my hands over my head, my koganzug transmitting signals through my hands to imitate the feel of rubbing my shaved hair with a bare hand.

"Don't you ever get tired of this?" I ask quietly.

Tired of what?

"Of fighting."

Fighting with you? If this is about when I tricked you into asking that woman for intercourse-

I sigh in exasperation. "Forget I asked."

I push off the wall, planning to go back into the banquet and check on my mark, when the door to one of the private rooms down the hall opens.

A Lowly waiter walks through it, adjusting her dress and smoothing her apron. She enters the hallway and walks in the opposite direction.

That's Agent Perchta, Thirteen says suddenly.

'What?' I subvocalize, shocked. 'How do you know?'

The way she walks.

Follow her, Kog Prime orders suddenly, startling me. The cold, articulate voice—still Thirteen's voice but easily distinguishable by its cadence—makes my hair stand on end. *Confirm order.*

'Order confirmed,' I subvocalize, my heart sinking.

This is why Devils can't trust. Not even me and Perri. We never know when we'll be ordered to betray each other.

I walk at a leisurely pace, giving Perri a chance to get ahead. It is the only form of protest I dare use. I might still get a flogging for it, but it shouldn't warrant a restoration. I don't want to betray Perri, but I can't risk a restore. Who knows what Kog Prime will erase if given the chance?

By the time I reach the lounge, Perri is gone from sight. Unless she suddenly disguised herself as one of the security guards, she's no longer in the building.

Considering Kog Prime's request, Perri must still have her dark mode permissions from her two weeks of undercover work; otherwise, Kog Prime could just follow her itself. Dark mode gives us access to our koganzug and auxiliary while isolating our koganzug's signal to prevent detection, consequently severing our connection with Kog Prime as well. That's also why I didn't feel a biomech surge when she walked into the hallway.

Perri uses this privilege to her full advantage. We never talk in specifics, but all Devils joined the Vogt military for a reason. From what I know of Perri, she's spent the last five years searching for someone. Has she discovered a new lead here?

'I've lost visual on the target. Any word on her location?' I ask Thirteen, knowing full well that Kog Prime wouldn't have asked me to follow her if she could be tracked.

Agent Leviatan, abort and return to your post, Kog Prime replies.

I smother a smirk. Good.

Leviatan, why didn't you follow orders? Thirteen asks, having waited until Kog Prime was no longer synced with our channel.

"I did follow orders."

You did, but you didn't.

"Just like when you gave me that wrong translation and tricked me into asking that woman for sex. You followed orders, but you also didn't."

So, you played a joke on Kog Prime?

"Sure." Yes, a joke. This is all a bad joke.

I return to the door that will get me closest to the

high table in the banquet hall. I reach for the knob.

Transmission from Captain Wolfsbann, Thirteen declares suddenly.

'Accept,' I respond, somewhat surprised. Did the Captain find something out about the terrorists? Or maybe he's going to reprimand me…

'Stay outside the door. We don't need you here,' he says. Then he ends the transmission abruptly.

What? I wonder in confusion.

Commence Phase Three of the operation, Kog Prime announces.

I freeze, understanding. The sounds of furniture crashing, glass shattering, and people screaming penetrates through the door in front of me. Explosions. The deep and hollow thuds of hand-cannons firing. The screaming increases. Something hits the door in front of me and I jump back.

A person shouts on the other side of the door, a man's voice. "Oh, gods, it's locked. It's locked!" He pounds the door with his fists. "Help us!" He screams. "Someone please open the door. Please!"

I reach for the knob.

Don't do it, Thirteen says. *You'll be violating orders.*

But...

You can't help anyway. What difference can one person make?

Not much, but...

You'll just get us killed.

It's true. I can't even protect myself. How can I protect someone else? anyone else? Least of all, everyone else.

I pull my hand away. The man on the other side of the door screams. The sound heightens, growing shrill, then suddenly cuts off.

The clamour of fighting and screaming and killing and dying continues. Blood spreads from beneath the door. I back away, my gorge rising, but I swallow it down, putting my hands over my ears and closing my eyes.

Leviatan, you seem to be in distress, Thirteen says.

Don't touch her, a voice says from my memories—

the same child's voice that asked if the elephant was real. Don't you dare touch her!

My head throbs with pain.

Agent Leviatan, Kog Prime says.

I cringe at Kog Prime's cold tone, but it severs the memory, releasing me from the pain.

You have been reassigned to complete Agent Perchta's tasks, Kog Prime continues. *You are to locate the hidden lab identified several days ago and collect all salvageable data before destroying the lab. Additional orders will be given after you complete this task.*

I turn away from the door and turn away from the memory. Then I run... Run from the door I was too much of a coward to open.

Chapter 4: Nightmare

As I run, I retrieve my Devil's mask from where it was hidden in my uniform and place it on my face. The biomechs of my koganzug shift and reach for the mask, fusing it into place.

Thirteen leads me back through the quiet streets of Bergverk toward the Great Gate. As I run, I tear off my uniform jacket and shirt and strip the pants, ripping the belt and fabric away. Beneath is my koganzug, the biomech skin has changed from skin-toned to satiny black.

I am Leviatan, the Devil of Envy. My devil's mask covers the lower half of my face, a grotesque maw of jagged teeth shockingly white against the black armour of my koganzug. The mask of the crocodile, a cold-blooded predator recorded in The Annals.

My koganzug armour is as cruel as it is powerful. The nodes where the biomechs are stored and maintained puncture my body like nails and anchor directly into my bones, and the kog port at the nape of my neck connects the system to my brainstem and spine. When the armour is deployed, the biomechs covering my skin pierce my flesh and attach to the muscles and nerves beneath.

In this way, my koganzug replicates my anatomy for Thirteen's use. As my auxiliary, he monitors my vitals, provides first aide and pain relief, and alters my armour to support my movements.

The koganzug is more than combat armour—it has become my flesh and bone, my muscles and tendons, even my eyes. The Devil's mask is not my disguise; it has become truer than my face beneath.

That's why I'll need to leave soon. I need to become human again before duty becomes nature.

Bergverk is quiet. The city began as a mining site. As the miners delved deeper into the mountain, their families moved into the abandoned shafts higher up. The mountain became a hive of life, but tonight it will become a tomb.

The houses are small and compact; their walls reach to the ceilings of the mines. Vents puncture the ceiling like skylights, showing the silhouettes of trees against the night sky. True to their heritage, rails for mining carts and handcars occupy the centre of the roadways and gas lamps illuminate the streets.

The night watchman carries a bird in a cage with him, checking for gas leaks as he walks the streets. When he sees me run by, he stares for a moment before scrambling away, running in the opposite direction. He leaves the bird screaming in its cage on the ground. I don't pass another soul due to the curfew.

I reach the train yard within minutes and pass through the city entrance into a maze of warehouses and train cars. The train cars are empty, the steam engines cold and silent in their bays. The warehouses are locked, the minerals and metals ready to ship after the peace negotiations end.

Nightmare

The Great Gate stands at the far end of the yard. Thirteen leads me off to the side, and I weave around stacks of crates waiting to be loaded onto the train cars. I turn a corner into a corridor that dead-ends where the wall of the Great Gate meets the mountain.

This should be where the entrance to the hidden laboratory is located.

I can't seem to catch my breath. I crouch and lean my back against the wall, pressing the heels of my hands into my eyes until phantom lights flash across my vision.

'Just give me a minute.'

One minute, starting-

"Let me rest!" I shout, the words making the metal sheds around me vibrate.

Understood.

I breathe out heavily, relieved, and lean my head back against the stone.

Realisation sets in. This operation isn't an assassination; it's a massacre. From what Bann said, I assumed we would take out the top leadership and then take in the orphaned officials. This though, this feels more like a cleansing, and not just of the Coalition Government.

How many sympathetic Vogt Faction members will die? And the Arkists? The Noah is probably already dead. How many more will be by the end of the night?

'Thirteen, how many targets were assigned for this operation?'

I... don't know.

'I expected as much. I thought there were 'targets,' but it's the entire city that's at risk.'

Why? Because Bergverk the last Coalition Stronghold?

I shake my head. 'No, I don't think the Vogt planned this, even if they'll still take advantage of it.'

The Great Houses and the Immaculates didn't arrange this. Those people merely dabble in politics and religion, taking sides as they see fit. The Arkist Church claims to be neutral in the war for control of the Reichland, but the Neo-Arkists have secretly allied with the Vogt Faction.

Why exterminate everyone at the banquet? Why risk getting the entire city involved? What are the people who planned this trying to hide?

Hide…

My thoughts come back around to my current mission. "It's because of the hidden laboratory. It's because of the secrets that the laboratory holds."

The one we're about to enter? According to Agent Perchta's data, there's a door in the rock face.

I shudder against Thirteen's sudden intrusion into my thoughts. 'What rock face?'

The one behind you. That's why you sat here, isn't it? You're just too stupid to know what to do next.

Yes, I think vaguely. I'm just too stupid to know what to do.

I turn around and examine the rock face, searching strata for a mismatch. I find it, a groove subtly concealed among the variations. Running my fingers along it, the biomechs register a texture and temperature differences of one side of the groove from the other. A false door.

I stab my hand into the groove, using my armoured fingers like a wedge. Stone and metal give way. I grip the metal, feel it warp around my fingers, and wrench the false door away from the cliff face, peeling it like a tin can, and toss the wreckage aside. All that's left is a gaping hole into the mountain.

'Laboratory entrance located,' I subvocalize. 'Entering.'

Thirteen transmits my report to Kog Prime.

I step into the darkness. My koganzug helps my eyes adjust to the gloom, but then the hallway comes alight from bulbs hanging from the ceiling. The bulbs flicker wildly, but it's the first time I've experienced lamps that come on by themselves. I thought only the Vogt had access to relics this advanced.

'Thirteen,' I subvocalize. 'Who runs this lab?'

According to the Agent Perchta's data, a Dr. Reuben Wilhelm.

'Who is he?'

His file is locked.

'But Kog Prime has declared him a traitor?'

Correct.

The hallway extends a few dozen meters and ends at a metal door. There are scuff and tears in the white paint of the threshold, indicating large loads being carried in and out from the train yard, and it smells of acrid cleaners and paint. I notice stains on the stone floor.

Blood stains, Thirteen reports when I crouch down and touch them.

'Can you identify what from?'

Human. And the blood stains are from different time periods.

So, either people got injured in this hallway often or people were the deliveries.

I stand at the metal door. A circular window, like a porthole, dominates the centre of it. I peer through cautiously, but the room on the other side is lit by only a dim, red glow. Thirteen can analyse what I see with better detail, but he can still only see what I see. I'll have to go in blind.

I take a deep breath and prepare myself for a fight.

Then I raise my hand behind me, fingers pressed together. A thin thread of biomechs extends from my fingers. I turn my hand and grip the thread, flicking it like a whip, and it shatters the bulbs over my head, plunging me into darkness. The thread quickly retracts back into my koganzug. At the same time, I dig my other hand into the metal door and wrench it open. It grinds on its track.

Nothing happens. No shouts of alarm. No blaring sirens. No gun shots, canon fire, or shattering glass. The lab is empty and in complete disarray.

Someone was here before me.

I step into the room, but no lights come on. The bulbs are shattered already. Only the dim red glow of the emergency lights illuminates the lab. Cages line one side of the room, each holding an animal. Four tables on wheels occupy the centre of the room, white sheets thrown over forbidding shapes on all of them save one. Broken shackles hang off the empty one.

A small office occupies the far side of the room, separated from this space by glass windows. A desk and konsole surrounded by bookshelves occupy that room, but the wall of windows is shattered and the books have been thrown to the floor. The konsole and screen have both been crushed.

I study the cages: whiptail rabbits, spined rats, urvogel hawks—all dead. The only enclosure that has movement is a large case housing what appears to be makerbugs. The tiny insects buzz around a small hive of pitted black stone. At the bottom of the cage is the corpse of a spined rat infected with blood rot. The makerbugs feed on the infected flesh. Whoever pillaged the place knew better than to mess with this cage. Getting swarmed by makerbugs is just as lethal as a plague blade.

'How long have the animals been dead?' I ask.

Not long. Rigor mortis has yet to set in. Let me test their blood.

I reach into a few of the cages and allow a small needle formed by my koganzug to pierce the animals.

They were poisoned by the same toxin. The most likely scenario is that someone was destroying the data.

I examine the room and note a scattered pyre of burned notebooks. Thirteen's theory appears true, but the fact that the pyre is scattered and the books are on the floor tell me they were interrupted.

My boots crunch on shattered glass. Noxious fumes rise from puddles of chemicals on the floor, but my koganzug filters the air for me.

I pull off one of the white sheets. A young female lies on the table, her body bare, wrist and ankle restraints shackling her to the table. Black veins of blood rot line her face and trace her body. Stitches extend from her collar bone to her pelvis. I place a hand gently on her forehead. Her body is already cold.

She is a hollowbern—she was not sick from blood rot. An autopsy was performed post-mortem, but there are signs of numerous surgeries performed while she was alive. The most probable explanation is that she was a test subject.

I nod in acknowledgment and gently place the sheet back over her.

I don't want to, but I carefully lift the sheets on the

other two tables. One is a young female approximately the same age as the other, but she is not hollowbern and had contracted blood rot. The other is an adult male who had contracted blood rot. They all bear signs of multiple surgeries performed while they were alive. Autopsies had been performed on the two females but not the male. Then there's the empty table with the broken shackles...

Live test subjects brought in through human trafficking.

Bergverk hosts a nightmare tonight but has hidden a nightmare for much longer.

His hands, Thirteen says.

One of the male's hands is frozen in a clenched fist while the other is open. I pry open the fist and find a lapel pin clenched in it, one of the small metal badges people at the banquet liked to sport on their suits. He had clenched it so hard that it gouged his palm.

I recognise the emblem on the pin immediately—an old man in a robe holding a giant key. It's the same symbol the Neo-Arkist leader was wearing at the banquet.

I stash the pin into my shoulder holster.

'Let me ask the Captain about this before you report to Kog Prime,' I subvocalize quickly.

I don't believe I can-

'Do your best to delay.'

I smell blood, Thirteen answers instead.

I check the room, but there's no blood. The bodies are clean despite the signs of surgery.

It's coming from the office.

I follow Thirteen's instructions and he guides me to a more private corner of the office not visible from the lab. A sleeping cot was thrown over and searched, and a set of lockers have been pried open and emptied. On the floor in front of one of the lockers is the body of a woman. Her feet extend into the locker like she was hiding there.

I check her pulse. There's nothing. I take a tissue sample for Thirteen to analyse.

That's strange, Thirteen says. *According to my post-mortem analysis, it appears she died after the test animals but before she entered the locker.*

'What?' I ask, surprised.

Look at her feet and ankles. They're broken but they didn't swell because she was already dead. Someone killed her and hid her in the locker.

'Can you identify her?'

Dr. Mia Kroff. She was one of the scientists stationed here. Cause of death: broken neck vertebrae and severed spinal cord. It appears she was assassinated.

'Was she on our kill list?'

No. In fact, she was to be captured alive for questioning.

I try to put the pieces together in my mind. 'So, someone came here and killed the scientist. Then they tried to destroy the lab's data but were interrupted?'

No, that cannot be correct. Whoever killed this scientist hid her body so we can conclude they did not want their intrusion to be noticed. The people who searched the lab did not care if their actions were noticed.

'Then there are several groups involved?'

Yes. I assume it was the scientist that began killing the test subjects and destroying records. However, it appears that someone killed her, hid the body, and left before she completed the process. Afterward, another group arrived, searched the place aggressively, and left before we arrived.

'You said the test animals hadn't been dead long and the scientist died after that, but wouldn't all these events have had to take place in the last few hours? How could the last group have left without running into me?' I examine the office more closely—the answer coming to mind without Thirteen telling me. 'There's another exit.'

I search the wrecked office. It takes only seconds to discover the hidden exit. The desk has wheels. I shove it and kick in the panel behind it. It buckles, hidden hinges tearing off, and opens into an unlit tunnel that curves out of sight.

Incoming transmission from Captain Wolfsbann.

'Put him through.'

Leviatan, stay where you are. I'm coming.

'Captain? But I'm fine. Why-'

Just say where you are.

The transmission ends abruptly.

I stand at the entrance of the tunnel, confused. 'Why does Captain Bann need to come here? Kog Prime assigned this mission to me.'

But it was originally Agent Perchta's.

A suspicion grows in me. I don't know Perri well, but of all the Devils, I know her best. We all have our reasons for becoming Devils, and Perri, she always seems to be looking for someone. She told me she specialised in espionage because she liked to spend extended periods in many different places. She often volunteers for additional missions but never in the same place twice.

Except for Bergverk.

This was her second operation in Bergverk in only a few months, and in the few days I'd been here, she had snuck out frequently. She seemed more cheerful, too. Now, Kog Prime reassigned her tasks and Captain Bann is coming.

Lights Above, why didn't I realise it earlier?

"Perri killed the scientist," I say, understanding all at once. "She found what she's been looking for so she's going to stop being a Devil. She wants to leave the Vogt." And the Captain isn't going to let her.

Against orders, I run into the tunnel.

Chapter 5: Music Box

The tunnel extends two-hundred meters or so, curving gently one direction and then another. At the end of it, I run out into a gloomy chamber lit with flickering lamps hung from the ceiling. Columns scattered throughout the room rise up from a stony floor and hold a ceiling of honeycombed arches. A dirt path worn into the mountainous floor winds around the columns.

The layout and architecture are vaguely familiar to me, and I know intuitively—that feeling again of having seen it somewhere before—that this chamber is hidden beneath an Arkist Church. The columns are the church's footings, and somewhere at the end of the trail will be a secret door leading up into the church's main chapel.

From the architecture and layout, it seems we are beneath Bergverk's Arkist Church, Thirteen confirms.

'I guessed as much. Then the Arkist Church is involved with the lab?'

It does seem unlikely that the lab could use this path for access and egress without the helmsman of this chapel noticing, but I thought the Arkist Church and the Vogt were friends now. Why are we supposed to destroy their lab?

I scoff loud enough for Thirteen to hear, just to annoy him, then shrug with false nonchalance. 'I told you before, not all Arkists. We allied with the Neo-Arkists, and tonight we helped them take over leadership of the Arkist Church.'

I think of the pin I found in the lab with the image of the old man with the key. Clara Neuseman, head of the Neo-Arkist movement, had worn the same thing to the banquet tonight.

Thirteen makes the connection at the same time I do. *And the Neo-Arkists? What part do they have in this?*

"A turncoat Vogt scientist heads up a lab in Coalition territory so it's no surprise the Vogt would raid the lab…," I subvocalize, thinking aloud to better define my thoughts.

Thirteen replies, his words an echo to mine. *The lab is located under an Arkist Church with a secret corridor leading out through the church, implying that the Arkist Church is connected to the lab…*

'But a Neo-Arkist lapel pin is found clenched in the hand of a dead test subject on the same night a massacre leaves the Neo-Arkists in control of the Arkist Church…'

And while the leaders of the Arkist Church were busy dying, someone was here trying to destroy the research.

I stop in my tracks.

"A cover-up," I whisper, as much to myself as Thirteen. When I continue, I subvocalize. 'The Neo-Arkists ran the lab without consent from the Arkist Church leadership or the Vogt. The Coalition may not have even known about it.'

That is possible. The helmsman of this specific congregation has strong ties to Clara Neuseman.

'The Neo-Arkists knew about tonight, knew the lab would get raided, so they got here first to destroy the research and evidence. They didn't want the Vogt to know what they've been up to. This operation isn't about ending the civil war; it's about someone's private agenda.' I feel sick. 'Thirteen, what if the peace negotiations were sincere? What if it was sincere and now we've wrecked it? All this bloodshed for nothing!'

You can't know that. We don't have enough evidence to support any of your conjectures.

I take in several deep, shaky breaths. 'Thirteen, I'd like to leave the Vogt after tonight. I'd like to leave with… with Perri." There, I said her name. "Do you think the Captain will let me?'

Thirteen answers with silence. They'll probably remove my hardware before I go. What does that mean for Thirteen? I doubt Kog Prime will destroy him. He'll probably be absorbed back into Kog Prime's main system, just like what should have happened to him for years.

'Any signs of Perri passing this way?' I ask.

Maybe I can convince her to resign officially and not just run? Having our koganzugs removed is probably as dangerous as having them implanted, but the hardware would be gone. No more voice in the head. No more immune korrectives to keep the implants from festering. No more people trying to kill us for our Devil's masks... I think it'd be worth the risk.

I wait quietly while Thirteen scans our surroundings. He analyses the images and sounds in minute detail, cross-examining them against his data logs of sights and sounds.

Breathing, he says, sounding surprised. *Here, in this chamber.*

'Not mine?'

Of course it's not yours. I'm not that ineffectual.

'Where?'

Thirteen guides me along the dirt path. It goes up and over a hill of stone, the columns short and the ceiling low here. I bow beneath it, cresting the hill, and find carnage on the other side.

Three bodies lie near the dirt path. Two wear the dark red garments of the Arkist Church. Of them, one wears the Neo-Arkist pin on his cowl, and on the other, there's a tear where the pin should have been. They must have helped the scientist destroy the lab.

I don't recognise the third body.

'Who is he?' I ask Thirteen.

According to my facial recognition analysis, he was one of the acrobat terrorists.

I grunt in surprise. This night keeps getting more twisted.

There's no blood on the bodies. Instead, the air smells of hot metal, the biting odour of a forge. But there's no forge or hot metal. There's only blood rot—three severe cases of blood rot where the bodies have broken down into Black Dust within minutes—the kind of blood rot caused by a plague blade.

Blood rot starts with the outer flesh and only stops once the corpse grows cold. That's the horror of the disease. The victims live through their decay—must endure the pain and horror of it—until it finally reaches enough organs to kill them. The infection caused by a plague blade is so rapid that the person may even experience their own face melting off before they die. Then, when they're dead and the body cools, the decay stops, leaving the desiccated remains.

I'm not sure which is worse, the slow decay of blood rot contracted from the environment, or the rapid decay of a plague blade wound.

All three are dead, Thirteen reports.

'And the breathing?'

A peal of laughter echoes through the chamber in answer, but there's no mirth in the laughter. My skin prickles beneath my armour.

"Perri?" I call.

Agent Leviatan, that laughter does not sound like mentally stable laughter.

A scream pierces the air, a shriek of despair that cracks and turns to cackles. A shudder runs down my spine. 'Is that Perri?'

I... I don't know. My sound analysis says yes, but...

Music Box

Yes. It is Agent Perchta.

Why does it seem like even Thirteen feels the fear? Like he can sense it, the wrongness.

Left! Thirteen shouts suddenly.

I spin to the right. A wickedly curved plague blade cuts the air where I stood, centimetres from my back. I turn, unsheathe my plague blade from its shoulder holster, and raise it over my head, catching one of Perri's karambit blades as she slashes down from above. Her daggers are short and curved, like claws meant for gutting opponents.

Our blades clash, and I notice a good third of one of her karambit blades has been broken off. I've never seen or heard of a plague blade getting broken. The only thing as hard as they are is another plague blade.

I throw Perri back just as she slashes with her other blade. She lands only a few meters away, crouched and ready to lunge. Her koganzug armour covers her face and shields her eyes. No feathery green dress or pink hair here. The armour covers her body in a black, satiny skin, serpent-like in its texture, but she's not wearing her Devil's mask. I can still see the contours of Perri's face, the contractions of her muscles, and her fierce scowl of wild anger.

"Perri, it's me!" I yell.

Her eyes narrow, but she doesn't relax her stance.

It's no use Agent Leviatan. She doesn't recognise you.

"Why! Why doesn't she recognise me?" I ask, but I'm not listening for an answer. "Perri-"

She screams and charges straight for me. Her behaviour is unlike any of our training; instead, it contains wild savagery, the intent to kill at all costs.

"Perri!" I shout, but she doesn't stop.

She doesn't recognise us! Kog Prime performed a restore. No, it's worse than that. Perri is not Perri anymore!

Thirteen is right. Perri is not Perri anymore. This creature is Perchta, one of the Vogt's Devils.

I dodge frantically, using my koganzug to dance around her crazed attack. She stabs at my stomach and slashes at my neck. I duck, but she kicks me in the side, throwing me into one of the columns. It shatters, chunks of stone landing on top of me. One smashes my hand, knocking my plague blade from my grasp.

She's coming! Thirteen warns.

Perri pounces on me. I punch her wrist, knocking one of the curved blades out of her hand, but she stabs with the other broken blade and presses down on it with her entire body. I grip her wrist with both my hands, stopping the broken tip of her plague blade from burying itself in my eye. She grips my shoulder with her free arm, trying to pull me into her blade. My arms tremble despite my koganzug. She snarls, teeth showing, her attention entirely focused on her blade.

"Perri, stop!" I shout.

But she slowly overpowers me, ignoring the toll her koganzug is taking on her muscles and tendons and the drain on her body's caloric energy. The broken end of her plague blade moves closer to my face; I'm watching my death in slow motion.

Hold steady, Thirteen cries. *Don't let her kill us. If you let her kill us, I'm holding you entirely responsible.*

Stupid, useless auxiliary.

I grit my teeth. "Perri, please," I plead. "I'm not going to hurt you. Please stop. It's Tantan! I'm Tantan!"

The pet name makes her pause. She at least turns her attention to where my face should be. I release the biomechs covering my face. They'll do little good against her plague blade anyway. The biomechs pull away to the sides of my head, dropping my crocodile Devil's mask to the stone floor and revealing my true face beneath. The same delicate lines and sharp features I wore at the banquet.

"See," I tell her. "Tantan. I won't hurt you."

She disengages her koganzug from her head, the biomechs peeling away, filing into the lower part of her suit, and for the first time, I see Perri's true face.

She's a hollowbern. Black streaks swirl across her skin like smoke, the veins small and delicate. The shaved hair on her scalp is a close-knit carpet of pink, and her eyes are a brilliant orange, the colour of sunset at harvest time.

Tears run down her cheeks. "It hurts, Tantan," she whimpers. "It hurts so much."

She still hasn't let go of her plague blade, and I still haven't let go of her wrists. The power is still there in her grip, bearing down on me. I don't dare relax.

"I did it. I didn't mean to, but I did." Tears run off her nose and drip onto my face. "I can't bear it!"

She screams again, that despairing shriek that I can feel in the pit of my stomach. I grit my teeth, ready for her to attack me again.

Suddenly, she flips her blade, pointing it towards herself. It catches me by surprise, and I don't have time to reverse my strength. She uses my own hands to stab herself. The only thing I can do is swerve to miss her heart. Her broken blade plunges into her chest, breaking her koganzug armour and piercing the flesh.

Her shriek cracks and turns into a cackle. I drop my hands, staring at the hilt of her plague blade.

Perri stands, weaving unsteadily on her feet and the plague blade still stuck in her chest. She turns away from me, like she's forgotten I'm there, and wanders from the path. She stumbles away, leaning on pillars for strength before carrying on. Infected by a plague blade, her koganzug begins to die. The biomechs flake off in chunks like bits of ash, burning up in a glowing trail of embers.

Shaken, I stand and follow her from a safe distance. She laughs softly as she stumbles between the pillars, a sound that echoes in the empty chamber. I've never heard such a sad sound.

She leads me around the side of an escarpment of stone. It creates a kind of cave on the other side. Hidden inside the cave is another corpse. Perri kneels beside the corpse, the embers of her dying koganzug falling on its already unrecognizable face. Blood rot has taken this person too, but its deterioration has progressed farther than the bodies of the Neo-Arkists or acrobat near the path. He was killed before them.

Perri caresses the half-decayed face, gore showing beneath a layer of Dust.

"I found him," Perri says, slurring. "I finally found him." The blood rot from her plague blade spreads to her face, and the flesh of her cheek begins to disintegrate.

The corpse lies on the ground in a foetal position, legs curled up near his chest and back curved. It appears to be male. He's tall and emaciated and was possibly a hollowbern. He wears very little, just a pair of ragged pants. Then I notice old surgery scars and new stitches on one of the few undamaged stretches of skin on his back, and I realise who he was. He was the man that occupied the fourth table in the lab. He is the reason Perri killed the scientist.

I kneel down on the other side of the corpse and realise he has something clasped to his chest. I recognise Perri's music box, and my chest constricts. It's her most precious item—a genuine relic dating back to the Origin War and passed down in her family for generations. She played the melancholy song often for me during the days after my installation surgery.

For Perri to give it to someone…

"Who was he?" I ask quietly.

"My reason," she answers. Her face twitches, the

muscles misfiring. "My reason," she repeats.

I understand. Her reason for everything. Her reason to live. Her reason to join the Devils. Her reason to kill. Her reason to leave. Now, her reason to die.

"Was he worth it?" I ask quietly.

Perri's muscle twitches worsen. I force myself not to look at her as her skin deteriorates, showing fat and muscle beneath. Her body trembles with the pain.

"I'm sorry," I whisper. "I shouldn't have…"

I shouldn't have cared, but I don't say it out loud. Saying it aloud makes it real. But if I hadn't cared, I wouldn't have come here to see if Perri was okay. I wouldn't have been the one to stab her.

Captain Wolfsbann is here, Thirteen says, his voice soft.

The Captain walks up behind Perri, his koganzug shimmering like it's just been cleaned, like he's already washed himself of the blood he spilled in the banquet hall. The plain uniform from the banquet is long gone, and his smiling wolf's mask looms over us. The mask covers his entire face so all I can see are his eyes glittering from within the holes in his mask.

Perri is too far gone to notice him.

"Captain," I say, my voice cracking. "You can save her, can't you? You always have antiserum. You can give it to her. If we give it to her now, she'll be okay."

"She's a double agent, Leviatan. A traitor. She was the one working with the terrorists. The attack was their diversion to extract her."

His voice is so cold, colder than I've ever heard before. It chills my blood. "She should be arrested then. She shouldn't die like this."

He cocks his head, an eerie sight with the smiling wolf's mask he wears. "Let her go, Leviatan. This is better for her."

"No, she can resign." I argue desperately, nonsensically even to me. "We'll get her patched up, do the court-martial, and she'll do her time and leave. She can go far away and just be Perri. She can be whatever she wants to be. Just give her the antiserum, Captain. Please…"

Captain Bann hesitates before he finally answers.

"No one leaves, Leviatan."

My breath catches. "But your friend… He resigned. He gave me-"

The Captain cuts me off ruthlessly. "He's dead. A Devil is either killed by their enemies or the side effects of their koganzug."

"But…" It feels like my lungs turned to stone. It's hard to breathe, hard to speak. "But you said-"

"You've spent five years in this hell, and you still believe that lie?" The Captain snorts in disgust. He points at Perri. "I told you that because you were just a kid, a kid stupid enough to enlist despite my objection, totally oblivious to what you actually got yourself into. You're old enough to know better now.

"Agent Perchta tried to leave so Kog Prime destroyed her mind, scrambled it into a primal state. Then Perchta killed her lover after going berserk. Leviatan, no one leaves."

Why? I want to ask. If you had told me the truth from the beginning, I never would have become a Devil. Instead, you told me stories that made yourself sound so glorious, righteous, heroic... You wove a fantasy and trapped me inside. Why did you lie?

But there's nothing I can say. There's nothing I can... There's nothing.

The Captain shakes his head. "If you won't let her go, I will."

He reaches over his head and grasps the hilt of his longsword. It measures nearly a meter long with a leather-wrapped hilt and the image of a blind-folded Lady Justice etched onto the blade. She stands atop words written in Manual: Ich schone niemand.

I spare no one.

Suddenly, Perri shrieks again, her brilliant eyes widening with insanity.

Leviatan, Thirteen shouts. *Get away from her!*

But it's too late; I'm too close.

Perri rips the plague blade out of her chest and lunges for me. At the same moment, a gleam of metal flashes across my vision. Perri freezes. Then her body slumps and falls to the side, landing heavily on her shoulder. Her head falls from her neck. Her blood slowly leaks onto the stone.

The Captain stands behind her, his executioner's blade wet with Perri's blood. At the sight, my endocrine enhancer engages, flooding me with dopamine—my comrade killed an enemy, and Kog Prime wants me to feel good about it.

I fold over and vomit.

That's when I begin to think… I think this is as far as I can go. No reason in the world can justify living like this.

It might be a lie, but one way or another, I leave tonight.

Chapter 6: Burning

I stare at Perri's headless body. The Ugly stirs in my belly, cold and hollow. "How did Kog Prime perform a restoration? There was no hard line connection to her kog port, and she was using dark mode!"

I turn my gaze to Bann. He wipes Perri's blood from his blade with his hand, concentrating, meticulous. Too meticulous.

"You did something, didn't you?" I ask accusingly.

Fake passcode, Thirteen says quickly, like he's worried he can't get the words out fast enough.

I scoff, the Ugly burning with cold, the pain searing and frozen in my chest. "You gave her a fake passcode," I answer for my captain. "You and Kog Prime made a trap for her. Her dark mode expired without her realizing, and Kog Prime wiped her mind."

Bann pauses in his meticulous care of his execution's blade. He's surprised I learned the truth. He returns his executioner's blade to his back, biomechs sheathing it, and stands straight and tall.

"You did this to her," I snarl, lashing out with my fist and the Ugly.

He bats my fist away. I strike with the other and he deflects it. I move faster, but his deflections and dodges keep pace with my strikes. The Ugly in me surges, makes my whole body feel cold and numb, but it gets no satisfaction. Finally, Bann grips my wrist, spins me to twist my arm behind my back, and then kicks the back of my knees. My legs collapse, wrenching my twisted arm.

"Bann," I say hoarsely, body bowed, "I owed her as much as I owed you."

"We never asked you to owe us," he answers softly, but when he continues, his voice firm and emotionless. "Agent Leviatan, you are being insubordinate. This is your only warning. Continue to act this way, and I will be forced to take punitive action."

"And you'll do what? Take my head off, too?"

"If I must," he answers coldly.

Perri's body is right in front of me, of course he would kill me, too. He knew Perri just as long. He worked with her just as closely. Look how she ended.

I hear the echo of Bann's words, 'No one leaves...' But Perri left... They always leave. When it comes to me, everyone leaves.

Please calm down, Thirteen begs. *If you keep going, you'll get both of us killed, and what will that prove? Keep quiet. Keep clam. Staying alive is the most important.*

The cold rage that fuelled my anger burns itself out. The ice in my veins retreats, and I feel my head clear. In its place is a mechanical rationality.

I know I'm just trying to cope—this is me taking emotions out of the situation so I can survive—but I can't help feeling like the Ugly me is more human than this unfeeling me.

I close my eyes, hide the sight of Perri's body.

Burning

Because I am a Devil.

"I understand," I answer, even though I don't. There is no understanding what happened here.

Kog Prime speaks, ending the clash. *Agent Leviatan, you have been assigned a new mission. Proceed to the Gauleiter's residence immediately to assist Captain Bann in dispatching one, Dr. Reuben Wilhelm.*

Bann releases me. Kog Prime probably alerted him to my new assignment at the same time it told me.

"I request for Agent Leviatan to be withdrawn from this operation and return to base," Bann says.

He's worried I'll run. He wants to force me into Kog Prime's clutches as quickly as possible.

A silent argument ensues between Bann and Kog Prime. Bann loses. He ends the communication with a tense look on his face. When Kog Prime speaks again, it's to both of us.

Dr. Wilhelm is a traitor to the Vogt der Wahrheit and knows secrets precious to the military and the Vogt. Taking care of this vulnerability is of utmost priority. Now, find Dr. Wilhelm.

Go. Fetch. Fight. Rip his throat out so I can pat you on the head and say 'good boy.' That's what Kog Prime means: you're not a man; you're a beast. I own you.

It's just like the Captain said—no one leave.

No, not Captain. He will never be my Captain again. He is Bann. The Vogt's Agent Wolfsbann. The Vogt's poison.

Blood smears his armour. His face is covered by the mask of a smiling wolf. He finishes wiping Perri's blood from his blade using the leg of his koganzug armour.

I retrieve my crocodile mask and return it to my face. My head armour deploys.

"Leviatan," Bann says, almost sounding regretful. "Just do what you're told."

I laugh in reply, a bitter spiteful sound that echoes in the dark chamber. Is this why Perri was laughing? What did Kog Prime do to make her laughter so broken and insane?

Bann and I follow the path out of the basement chamber and take a winding staircase up to the main chapel of Bergverk's Arkist Church. As we exit the church, Bann and I part ways, him taking one road and me another.

The Gauleiter's mansion is located in the uppermost cavern, Thirteen says.

"Why didn't you tell me Bann was coming to kill her?"

I didn't know. Even if I did, there are some things I cannot say.

"Like no Devil has ever been allowed to leave? It's been seven years, Thirteen, and you never gave me a clue."

I was strictly prohibited from informing you of this fact, as were all the other Devils. Why Kog Prime demanded so much secrecy for this matter, I do not know.

To keep me here; to make sure I stayed of my own volition for as long as possible. But why? I'm not a talent. Bann has had to complete a number of my missions. Considering how calculative and ruthless Kog Prime is, why not dispose of me? Or better yet, let one of Manny's apprentices kill me and gain a new, capable, willing Devil?

During the time, I've been in the hidden laboratory and beneath the church, the fighting at the banquet spilled into the city like I worried it would. Bergverk is burning and the people are burning with it.

Bergverk passes like a charcoal drawing—the main thoroughfare clouded with smoke, carnage on the steel cart track, and shattered glass on the stone. Each place punctuated by bodies. Each body marked with wounds inflicted by my comrades. There will be no Bergverk after tonight.

No one ever leaves.

But everyone always leaves.

Communication from Captain Wolfsbann, Thirteen reports.

"Ignore it," I reply.

Captain Wolfsbann is your commanding officer. You cannot ignore it.

Then why ask? Why pretend like I have a choice? Why do they keep pretending like I have a choice?

Burning

"Connect me."

'Leviatan,' Bann says, Thirteen transmitting his voice, 'don't do anything rash.'

The image of Perri's headless body flashes through my mind. I still feel empty, numb, but my breathing trembles and I clench my jaw.

I reach the Gauleiter's mansion. The Gauleiter was the political head of Bergverk and a vassal of the Coalition Government. He died at the banquet tonight, courtesy of Manny.

Like its master, the Gauleiter's mansion has become a corpse. It stares blankly at me, a skull-faced building with a blackened doorway. Fire has scorched the entire structure and continues to burn in the west wing. Several meters above the smouldering roof, smoke billows and collects against the cavern ceiling, searching for shafts and escape.

I follow a neatly paved path that meanders through ornate rock gardens and statuary. A few islands of plants sit below the shafts, using them as skylights. There are corpses among the stones and statues. The

Vogt had people stationed at the mansion in preparation for tonight.

I approach the mansion. The heavy double doors at the front entry are splinters and ash. Inside, the marble floors are scorched, the priceless draperies and furniture nothing but cold pyres. There are corpses in the main entry too.

After a long silence, Bann speaks again. 'I warned you. You could have joined another branch of the Vogt or worked as private security, but you insisted.'

Yes, I insisted. I didn't know anything so I insisted.

"Did Perri already know that no one can leave the Vogt?" I ask, standing at the threshold of the mansion.

'Yes,' he answers.

"And she tried to leave anyway?"

'Yes. Shows how much that man meant to her.' Then, more quietly. 'We both know I did Perri a favour.'

I can't think of a retort. Was Perri's death for the best? She joined the Devils for that man, suffered for years, and died for him. What was the point of all that suffering? She should have forgotten him. If she'd left him, then she never would have joined the Devil's in the first place.

Perri and I were alike in that way—keeping what we should leave and leaving what we should keep.

Bann gets back to business. He always does. 'The traitor took a secret passage out of the Gauleiter's mansion. I went to the exit to head him off, but he never appeared. I suspect the bastard turned around. I am following the secret passage toward the mansion, but I need you at the entrance waiting for him.'

"And then?"

He snorts. 'Kill him, of course.'

"Fine," I reply, and Bann ends the transmission.

I take a deep breath, steadying my nerves and preparing for this final act. Then I step over the threshold and into the Gauleiter's mansion.

Chapter 7: Wilhelm

The upper floor burned and collapsed, but the main floor is made from stone, even the support beams for the second story, so the walls hold true and carry the debris well. The Gauleiter was smart and wanted to be sure his path to the secret passage wouldn't be blocked by wreckage should something happen. Too bad he was at the Banquet Hall when the massacre began.

I follow the path of least resistance, taking hallways with the least debris. He planned his escape well, just not his survival.

At the end of a hall toward the back of the mansion, I find a door—the only door still intact. Metal glints beneath the scorched wood veneer. I place a hand on the door, and to my surprise, it pushes open. The door is unlocked—not even fully closed. It swings wide, as if in welcome.

A ticking sound draws me in.

Aside from the smell of smoke, the room appears untouched by the fire. A grandfather clock stands in one corner, the source of the ticking sound. Beside it, a tall window, glass panes still intact, and a four-poster bed beside it. A painting hangs above the headboard, an abstract piece made with the broad strokes of a palette knife.

A Schaafer painting? Palette knife was a hallmark of his. I take a closer look at it.

"Is that real?" I ask Thirteen.

It is, he answers. *It's worth several million marcs. Want to take it? There's no one who will mind at this point.*

A short, mirthless laugh escapes me. I never thought I'd see a Schaafer relic in person. Only five have ever been excavated.

I stare at the painting, a yellow monochrome. In the blotches and strokes of yellow and white, I see a flat-roofed house half-buried in sand. Shutters shield the windows, but the backdoor is open, a black rectangle amidst the blinding yellow. It swings in the wind, slamming against the house. I can hear it, the creak and bang as it hits the doorframe.

"Please, take a seat. I'll be done in a moment," a voice says, jarring me from my stupor.

I turn. The other side of the room extends into a sitting area, and there sits a small man writing at a large desk.

I glance at the painting again, but it's nothing but yellow and white paint smeared thick and wild over the canvas. No house. No door.

I turn back to the man who spoke. He hunches over a sheaf of paper, shoulders narrow, face thin, and hands soft like a child's. Glasses perch on the end of his sharp nose. He wears a jacket in the Reichlander style, loop buttonholes and a standing collar, but the jacket gapes open and buttons are missing. There's blood on the white shirt underneath.

Target acquired, Thirteen says suddenly. *Permission*

to execute.

I'm unsurprised. Somehow, it seems fitting that this man is Dr. Wilhelm.

The phrase 'permission to execute' triggers a physical response in me. After so many years of my endocrine enhancer rewarding me for executions, my body has started to anticipate it. With a bit of hormone manipulation, they turned murder into a craving.

But a thought occurs to me, allows me to hesitate. This man couldn't have known Bann was waiting for him. What was so important that he came back after escaping?

Wilhelm finishes writing, caps his pen and sets it aside. Carefully, he folds the pages into thirds, creases them with delicate fingers. Ink stains the side of his left hand. He inserts the pages into an envelope and presses a wax seal to close it. Then he holds the envelope in his hands and gazes at it, his expression thoughtful.

"In Amira, they say light is the left hand of darkness," he says. His eyes continue to study the sealed envelope. "In the Reichland, the Arkists believe the Sky People battle Darkness in the Lights Above. In Endonia, the sages teach all things do, and must, consist of light and darkness. What do you think, Leiden of the Dustlands?"

Hearing my true name should surprise me. It's been how long? Seven? Eight years since I last heard it? Besides, how does he even know it's me? My face is covered by my crocodile mask.

But, I'm beyond surprise. Kog is triggering my endocrine enhancer, driving up my anxiety and aggression to convince me to kill this man. What room is there for surprise?

"How do you know my name?" I ask.

"I know it because I'm the one who took it from you."

My thoughts are thrown back to those first weeks after my surgery when I knew nothing but pain and my call sign. I had contact with only three people, Perri, Bann, and the surgeon.

I take a seat in one of the ornate sitting chairs opposite the desk. "You're the surgeon... the one from the beginning. One of the Vogt's top scientists."

"Yes, but didn't the Kognitive Primary already tell you that?" He finally looks up from the envelope.

His eyes are grey-blue with the creaseless lids common in Endonia. His unmarked skin tells me he's an Immaculate. Makes sense. It's always one of them in charge of these types of projects.

In my experience, the most pure-blooded humans exhibit the least humanity.

"You know about Kog Prime?" I ask.

Even if this man is the Vogt's top scientist, Kog Prime didn't like getting talked about. Few people aside from koganzug users know about it, and we're not allowed to say anything about it without backlash from our endocrine enhancers.

"Yes, I know," he says. "I know just about everything: koganzugs and biomechs, biomech transfusions and software updates, kognitive auxiliaries and endocrine enhances for psychological conditioning, restorations, even the development of special abilities." He sets the letter flat on the desk and spins his chair toward me. "I know about you, Leviatan, and about Bann..." He lets that name linger a moment, like he expects me to react. When I don't, he continues, "...and about your comrades—Mammon, Perchta, even the Commander. I know all about it because I helped build all of it."

I grip the wooden arms of the chair. No wonder Kog Prime wants him dead. I close my eyes and sigh. "And are you a traitor?"

"Yes."

"Did you divulge the Vogt's secrets to unsanctioned parties?"

"I did."

I smile, eyes still closed. "Praise the Lights Above."

Agent Leviatan, Kog Prime interjects.

Kog Prime has been listening... Of course it has been listening. A rash fool is speaking with its most knowledgeable enemy.

You are due for psychological assessment and rehabilitation. Please report to a Vogt military clinic. Agent Mammon will proceed with this operation in your stead.

There it is, the order I've been waiting for. I was never surviving tonight without a neural restoration. Maybe it's because of what happened with Perri, or maybe it's because I now know the truth that no one can leave? Who knows? Maybe I already knew all this and was restored before so I'd forget it? How many times has this scenario repeated in the last seven years?

Agent Leviatan, you are to report to the nearest Vogt facility immediately, Kog Prime orders again.

This time, it triggers my endocrine enhancer to produce panic, and the Ugly stirs in the pit of my stomach. If I obey, the cortisol will give way to dopamine and endorphins, but I grit my teeth and breathe deeply.

"Go to hell, Kog Prime," I snarl between my teeth.

Dr. Wilhelm studies me. He can't possibly have heard Kog, but those blue-grey eyes look pensive. He leans forward, places his elbows on his knees, and steeples his fingers. "If I'm not mistaken, you hate the Vogt as much as I do."

His words set me off like a trigger. I laugh, then jump up from my seat and grab the arms of Wilhelm's desk chair. I put my masked face right up to his. Wilhelm leans back into his seat and stares, his eyes locked on my crocodile smile. The blood drains from his face.

"Hate the Vogt?" I snap. "Didn't I choose to become a Devil?" I shake my finger thoughtfully, like I've just realised something. "But no, I didn't really have a choice, did I? It was a trap from the beginning—a trap you helped set."

The Ugly gets the best of me, and Kog Prime tries to use it. The arms of his chair groan and splinter under my grip. I wrestle down the urge to kill him, to get it over with. But it's too soon. Once I kill Wilhelm, it will be the beginning of the end.

I snort derisively and stand straight. Wilhelm sags in relief, though he tries to hide it.

"I can't leave," I tell him, turning away. "I can never leave. From the moment Bann brought me to the Vogt, there was never a chance for me to be anything but a

Devil."

I relax my fisted hands, flex them wide, shake them out, and force myself to sit in the chair across from Wilhelm again. I lean my head back and close my eyes, wishing I could hear the normal sounds of Bergverk again—the rattle of carts on the rails, merchants and workers calling, children playing in the lanes, the deep rumble of blasts in the mines—but there's only silence and the heavy stench of smoke.

"Help me," the scientist murmurs.

My eyes snap open. "What?"

"Help me escape."

Pieces fall into place—things I've been trying to make sense of all night. "Perri was supposed to meet you, wasn't she? She was your way out of this mess... and you were hers. The acrobats were a diversion so she could raid the lab and get you out."

Wilhelm's silence is confirmation enough. He looks like he's not sure what to say. Maybe he thinks any response will get him killed... Maybe it will.

"What happened to her?" he finally asks.

"Bann chopped her head off," I answer curtly.

"I am sorry for your loss."

"Sure you are," I snap. "She was supposed to meet you but never arrived. That's why you came back. Why did she agree to help you?"

He sighs. "I offered her what she dearly wanted—to have her koganzug extracted."

I sit up sharply and stare at him. "You can do that?"

He smiles, but it's full of exhaustion and apology. "Theoretically, yes. And who better to try than the man who implanted it?" He grows thoughtful again. "Will you do it in her stead? Will you try to help me escape and I'll try help you removed your koganzug? It might kill you—I've never done it before—but at least it's a chance. If you keep me alive, I'll do whatever I can."

Don't do it, Thirteen begs, disregarding Kog Prime's surveillance for once. *Leviatan, if we obey right now, immediately, we won't even need a restoration. Being a Devil isn't so bad, right? We get good food and nice clothes; lots of people love us...* If Thirteen could sob, he would. His voice is high and whining.

"Shut up, Thirteen," I answer softly. "There's more to being human than food and drink. But how would you know that? You're just code and hardware."

Now it's Kog Prime's turn. *Agent Leviatan, this is treason. You will be terminated if you agree.*

I could question Wilhelm's sincerity or skill, but isn't Kog Prime's threat a confirmation of the offer's validity? Not to mention that Perri was willing to put her life on the line for this deal.

I smile widely. Today must be my lucky day. How often do I get a chance at treachery?

I extend a hand for Wilhelm to shake. "Deal."

Kognitive Auxiliary 013, suspend all jobs and prepare for reclamation.

"Reclamation?" I mutter in surprise. I've never heard the term before.

Wilhelm looks up sharply. "Dark mode. Initiate dark mode!"

I try but nothing happens. "My koganzug isn't responding."

Pain stabs through my head. It throbs behind my

eyes, like my brain is being crushed against my skull. Then memories disappear, leaving a void that rings in my ears.

A restoration without a hard line connection to my kog port, just like what Kog Prime did to Perri. Kog Prime plans to turn me into the beast it's always believed me to be.

Chapter 8: Letters

"No…" I breathe.

If Kog Prime performs a restoration on me now, I'll never be able to leave. Why can't I leave? I just want to disappear—to live like I never existed. That would be better than surviving like this. "No, no, no…"

The pain sears, a burn that goes deeper and hotter until even the nerves are dead, leaving behind a terrifying void. There's no coming back from this. I'll become the monster I always feared I'd become.

The pain stops suddenly.

"Initiate dark mode now," Wilhelm orders.

His voice sounds loud in the absence of pain. I stare at him. He sits at his desk with a device in his hand. It looks like a pen, but his thumb has mashed the button at the top of it and no pen tip has appeared.

He glares. "Now. You have about seven seconds." His tone broaches no argument.

"Kognitive Auxiliary 013, initiate dark mode," I say, voice hoarse.

Kognitive Auxiliary 013, initiating dark mode. Please provide the passcode, Thirteen replies.

"I don't have it." I speak aloud for Wilhelm's benefit, glancing at him.

"Three seconds," he says.

Agent Leviatan, you have ten minutes to provide the dark mode passcode issued by your superior officer or dark mode will be overridden.

I grind my teeth in aggravation. "Just do it!"

Dark mode initiates, closing off all signals to or from my kog port and cutting off contact with Kog Prime.

I gasp with relief. "Thirteen, koganzug status."

Koganzug 013, report: dark mode initiated, power reserve at--

"End report," I mutter.

My hands clasp the kog port installed in the back of

my neck. A hand grips my shoulder gently and I look up. Wilhelm stands beside me. He drops his hand, and I lean back in my seat.

This is bad, Thirteen mutters. *This is very, very bad.*

"What did you do?" I ask Wilhelm, indicating the device in his hand.

He looks at it and sighs, stuffing it back into the inside pocket of his jacket and returning to his seat. "A signal jammer. I hoped to save it for later, but..." He shrugs.

You just pissed Kog Prime off! Thirteen screeches. *After this, there's no way it will let us off. You just ruined us all!*

"Kog Prime burned me first," I snap in reply.

You deserve it, aligning yourself with a traitor. What were you thinking?

What was I thinking? I was thinking about Perri and her lover and about that hollowbern kid who joined the rebels and about Bann who had to kill him because I couldn't...

I lean my head back, trying to forget the pain I was

in only moments ago. "I have less than ten minutes to live. What now?"

Wilhelm shakes his head. "Reclamation doesn't kill you."

I close my eyes. "What is it then?"

"Kog Prime overheats your neuron network, causing brain damage to the part of your brain where memories are stored."

That must be what happened to Perri. Her dark mode expired and Kog Prime 'reclaimed' her.

"If it has that kind of ability, why doesn't Kog Prime just kill me?"

I hear Wilhelm sigh. "I don't know. Does the answer really matter at the moment?"

"No, not at the moment," I answer, but Kog Prime has a way of making things matter later. I open my eyes and stare at the ceiling.

Agent Leviatan, you have nine minutes to provide the dark mode passcode issued by your superior officer. Thirteen interjects, using his most robotic of voices.

I roll my eyes. "Thirteen, mute the countdown."

Unable to comply.

"Fine, then delay the countdown to the last five minutes."

I said I am unable to comply, he snaps.

I suppose this is Thirteen's equivalent to 'shove off.' I sigh, not looking forward to the incessant reminders of impending doom.

"Less than nine minutes, that's all we have before I have to power down." I tell Wilhelm. "Where to?"

He leans forward and eyes me appraisingly. "Rettung."

"The port city across the mountains?"

Wilhelm sits back and appraises me like he's just issued a dare. I hold his gaze.

"That's a long way."

"It is."

"And your family?"

He smiles sadly, picking up the letter on his desk and caressing the edges of it. "That long ways away. One of many reasons I need to reach Rettung."

I spend a long moment considering. It will be hard to

leave the Reichland—the Vogt closely monitors the pass through the mountains for terrorists—but tonight will create a lot of chaos on the border. Once we pass into Giya, we'll be much safer. The Vogt wants to conquer Giya and obtain its ports, but thus far, the desert has had too many spines for the Vogt to close its fist on it.

Thirteen issues another notice.

"Eight minutes," I inform Wilhelm.

Determination hardens Wilhelm's expression. "Get us clear of Bergverk. I'll take care of things after that, and I won't forget our deal."

Rettung, it is. I climb to my feet. "Then it's time to go."

Wilhelm slips on a satchel. The strap crosses over his shoulder and chest, and the bag hangs against his hip. He fiddles with the strap, adjusting his jacket beneath it, and then slips the letter into the satchel along with another letter he takes from the desk.

Then Wilhelm strides to the bed and climbs atop it. He lifts away the Schaafer painting, revealing a heavy door with a metal hand wheel at its centre. He starts to crank the hand wheel.

Just as Wilhelm finishes cranking the hand wheel, my biomechs surge. There's another koganzug user nearby. Wilhelm wrenches the hand wheel one last time.

"Wilhelm, wait!" I shout.

Too late. The heavy door explodes open, kicked in from the other side.

Chapter 9: Threads of Fate

I reach out an armoured hand, thick strands of biomechs extending from it to Wilhelm. They wrap his torso and shoulders, and I jerk him away from the door just as it explodes into the room. His head snaps forward, and he hits the floor hard in front of me, groaning. I pull the biomechs back into me and they merge with my koganzug again.

Bann stands in the entrance to the secret passage, having kicked the door off its frame. His koganzug is still stained with Perri's blood. Aside from the hand-cannon strapped to his waist, he wears his executioner's blade on his back and his wolf-faced Devil's mask.

Bann reaches over his head to grip the enormous sword. His koganzug releases it and he props it against the wall, the pommel nearly reaching his shoulders. He doesn't need it for this fight. In truth, he doesn't need it for any fight.

The reason Bann gave me his comrade's plague blade instead of keeping it for himself is because he has something more effective at his disposal in a fight against koganzug users. A biomech plague.

All Devils work to hone our manipulation of the biomechs, like my ropes and Perri's disguises, but Bann's skill is beyond us. His biomech poison plague is why he is the captain, both a leader and an enforcer for the Vogt.

I stare at him, mouth dry and breath caught in my throat. After seven years under his tutelage, I should have realised he wouldn't wait in the passage.

"I'm leaving, Bann," I tell him.

Wilhelm slowly gets to his feet to stand beside me. He grips the strap of his satchel tightly, knuckles white. My own pulse is racing.

Bann sits down in the doorway of the escape tunnel, his feet dangling several centimetres above the floor.

"You know what your problem is, Leviatan?"

He kicks his legs like a kid, banging his heels on the wall. "You never commit. You're always looking for a backdoor, an easy way out, somewhere you can run when things go wrong. Your fear of failure is a self-fulfilling prophecy."

I finally take a breath and try to steady my nerves. Can't let my voice tremble. "I just want to make my own choice. Have you ever made a decision that was all your own and not an order?"

Bann hops down from the doorway. "I have, and I won't make that mistake again."

Bann triggers his poison plague ability. The biomechs on his hands swarm over one another, like insects. The motion seems to make his hands shiver. If he touches me, his biomechs will transfer a virus to my biomechs, triggering them to self-destruct. The chain reaction causes self-immolation. Even if Kog Prime wants me alive, how long will Bann let me burn to punish me?

I put Wilhelm behind me, muttering for him to stay

close, and back us toward the bedroom door.

Adjusting biomech configuration, Thirteen informs me.

"I thought you weren't going to help," I mutter.

Given a choice between dying now or dying later, of course I will choose later. I am not stupid like you.

Fair enough.

Within milliseconds, the biomechs of my koganzug shift—more armour here; greater musculature there. Thirteen can tell we're in for a brawl.

"I don't want to fight you, Bann," I say.

He shrugs, walking toward me. "Want has nothing to do with us. We do what we're told."

He leaps at me, jumping over the bed, but I don't dash for the bedroom door like he expects. Instead, I lash the scientist to my back using biomechs and dive beneath Bann. Wilhelm shouts in surprise. Bann hits him, but there's little power in the strike, and his plague has no effect on Wilhelm. I'll have to apologise to Wilhelm for using him as a human shield later.

Bann lands heavily, a knee to the floor, in the spot

where we stood. I slide to a stop on my belly a meter or two from the secret passage. I unlash Wilhelm and toss him up to it. He scrambles through but waits just beyond the threshold.

Less than six minutes left. Where did the time go?

I draw my plague blade, separate it into two daggers, and face Bann. His attention jumps between me and Wilhelm; he's torn between fighting me and going after his target. If I can incapacitate Bann in the next few minutes, I should be able to carry Wilhelm to safety before I have to power-down.

Another biomech surge shivers through my koganzug, and Manny appears in the doorway behind Bann. He wears his favourite brown leather trench coat, flesh-coloured armour, and his hyena mask. The mask covers the upper half of his face, displaying a smiling top row of teeth and exposing his pointed jaw and thin lips that smile cruelly.

The Gods Below are not taking the least bit of pity of me tonight.

Dread seizes me.

"Took you long enough," Bann says. "Kog Prime wants him alive."

Manny's thin mouth curls into an ugly grin. "No need to worry. You know I don't like to rush things, Bann."

Even though I can't see Bann's face, I can sense his disapproval. Bann plays the rogue, but there's honour beneath it. Agent Mammon, on the other hand, likes to play with his food.

Manny flexes his hands. The biomechs form one hand into a cudgel and the other into razor-like claws. He might not have a plague blade, but his claw technique is nearly as brutal.

Bann nods at the secret passage. "Get the scientist. I'll take care of this one."

"Only if I get his plague blade," he snaps.

"Deal," Bann replies coldly.

Manny's smile widens. I can only imagine how his endocrine enhancer is making him feel. The man is addicted to murder.

See, Thirteen says. *Captain Wolfsbann doesn't want*

us dead. We should just give up.

"Do you think Manny will leave us alone if I just give up?"

No, but only you feel pain. I don't. As long as he keeps us alive, that's a good deal, right?

"Let me make this clear, Thirteen," I snap. "I make it out alive tonight, or I die trying with or without your help. Which do you prefer?"

Alive. I always prefer alive.

Of course you do. That's why you and I can never understand each other.

I glance at the secret passage, see Wilhelm still standing in the shadows. "Run, Wilhelm."

I don't get a chance to say more.

Manny sprints for the passage. With my free hand, I spool out strands of biomechs, wrap them around the sitting chair and swing it at Manny. The impact throws him into the far wall. He climbs to his feet smiling, rolls his shoulders and shakes out his arms, probably stalling while his koganzug reconfigures.

I charge at him, feigning a lunge with my dagger and

grab the post of the bed instead. The feint works. Manny dodges and I use the bed post to leverage my legs and kick him in the chest. He crashes through the wall and into the hallway.

The bed post snaps and I land on my side. It knocks the breath from me, but I don't have time to gasp. I roll and Bann's fist strikes the floor. The hit shatters the planks and sprays splinters. I roll to my feet and out of range of his hands, daggers held in a downward position. We stare each other down, breathing hard. He wears the face of a wolf, and I wear the face of a crocodile.

"Bann, escape with us!" I try, desperate.

He laughs, but there's no mirth in his eyes. "Escape? There is no escape, and trying only brings more pain. To you and to anyone you care about." His hands begin to shiver again.

I glance at the secret passage. Did Wilhelm make it out?

I turn my attention back to Bann. "How can there be more pain than this? We destroyed an entire city, Bann.

If there's even a chance to escape, I'm taking it."

Bann blocks the entrance to the escape tunnel. "You will never escape this, Leviatan. There's no undoing what we've done." He takes a few steps forward.

He's cornering me, I realise. I back away from him, terror lodged in my throat. "I know that."

"No, you don't," he replies. "If you did, you wouldn't be trying to escape. We're devils, Leviatan. After what we've done, that's all we can ever be."

Bann takes a battle stance, shivering fists raised and knees bent, weight shifting to the balls of his feet. His eyes narrow with killing intent behind his mask.

Four minutes. The time is passing faster than I can keep track.

The wall to my right explodes. Manny comes through it from the hall. His shoulder takes me hard in the ribs. Sparks explode where our koganzugs meet. Plaster and slivers of shiplap spray the room. Me and Manny go down in a heap. One of my blades is knocked from my hand, but I keep a tight grip on the other.

Threads of Fate

Manny grabs me from behind, his clawed hand digging deep into my shoulder near the collarbone, and his cudgel fist hammering that same spot on my ribs where his shoulder hit. Biomechs flake off my koganzug and burn out like sparks. Bruised flesh peaks from between fractures in the armour. Thirteen is forced to convert musculature to armour to shore up the fractures.

I wrench to the side even though it forces his claws deeper and stab blindly at Manny behind me. My plague blade meets armour. The armour resists for a moment before the blade disrupts the biomechs, forcing them to part, and slips into the breech.

Manny yelps and beats my wrist with his cudgel. I try to hold on and force my blade just a fracture deeper, but my armour fractures and my wrist breaks, forcing me to drop my dagger before it pierces Manny's flesh.

Thirteen braces my wrist, but I'm quickly using up my biomechs. Not that it matters. I have only minutes left to fight anyway.

I reach over my head with both hands and wrap a

biomech cord around Manny's throat and heave him over my shoulders, flinging him across the room. His claws jerk free from my shoulder and he hits the bed, shattering it.

Manny stands slowly, laughing. I pick up my daggers again and brace for another charge, but his eyes flick to the escape tunnel, and I realise I gave him a clear path to Wilhelm. He dashes for the entrance.

Cursing, I lunge for him, but Bann strikes first. He jabs at my head and body, less concerned about strength than he is about landing a hit and infecting my biomechs with his plague. I dance around the jabs like a fool, hips and shoulders swinging and jerking to avoid his hands, blocking with my daggers. He doesn't give me time to counter. It's a good thing he trained me or I'd already be dead.

I spot an opening and wrap one of his ankles with a biomech cord, jerking it out from under him. He goes down, but I don't let go. Thirteen adjusts my musculature, knowing what I want to do. I swing Bann from one side of the room to the other. He slams into the desk. Wood and paper erupt from the shattered drawers and ink splatters the wall. I whip the rope in the other direction. He shouts as he's flung to the other side and hits the grandfather clock. Its chimes clatter as it collapses around him.

Bann reaches toward his ankle, and his shivering hand touches my biomech rope. The swarming biomechs spreads from his fingers and ripple up my rope, but I detach it before the plague reaches me. The rope collapses into individual biomechs that explode like firecrackers.

Detaching like that costs me a lot of biomechs. Now, even if Thirteen converts all my biomechs to armour, there aren't enough to create sufficient layers, and I doubt Kog Prime will let me get a transfusion anytime soon.

I get out now or never, I decide. I run for the escape tunnel, twisting my daggers back into a single blade. I must have caught Bann off guard. He stands flat-footed in the wreckage of the clock as I grip the doorframe and heave myself up into the passage.

Pain pierces through me, radiates from the weak point Manny created in my side. I look down. A pole of metal protrudes from my side. It takes me a moment to realise it is a bell from the grandfather clock. Bann threw it like a javelin.

Leviatan... Leviatan... Thirteen tries to say something. I can't hear him over the blood rushing in my ears—probably a reproach for getting hit—but he interrupts himself to tell me there are only two minutes left.

Shock and pain hold me in place. Bann walks up to me and rips the metal javelin out of my side. My koganzug tries to create a compress, but it's a big wound. A lot of blood...

My plague blade falls from my fingers, and my grip on the doorway slips. I fall back into the room onto the wreckage of the bed. I clasp my hands over the wound, but it doesn't really matter at this point. Blood seeps between my fingers and runs down my side. The rushing in my ears makes it hard to hear, but I still catch the sound of rubble scraping underfoot. I look up to find Bann standing over me.

I wait for him to strike, expecting to feel his grip on my throat or a hand pressed gently to my chest because that's how Bann does things. Then the biomechs will surge and burn, searing deep into my flesh before they explode.

But he doesn't put the plague in me. He stands over me, waiting, and I realise he's going to take me back. He's going to drag me to a Vogt facility and let Kog Prime have me.

My pulse quickens. I don't want to go back. Please don't make me go back... I'd beg, but no words will come out of my mouth.

Singing echoes out from the escape tunnel and draws both our gazes. Manny appears out of the shadows dragging Wilhelm by the leg behind him.

Manny bellows a folk song, one somehow familiar to me. I know the words but not the memory connected to them.

> "Ribbons to a rope,
> Anchored to the weight of hope,
> Becomes like time..."

At the threshold, Manny throws Wilhelm into the room, and the man hits the floor and doesn't move. Manny cackles, leaving his song unfinished.

Bann retrieves his sword and draws it from its scabbard. The words and the image of Lady Justice etched onto it flash brightly before my eyes.

Less than one minute, Thirteen tells me.

Manny hops down from the escape passage, goes to Wilhelm and grips him by the back of his jacket. Wilhelm groans and Manny gently pats his face.

"Wakey wakey," he croons.

Wilhelm opens his eyes. He sees me laying in my own blood with Bann standing over me, and he smiles with sad resignation.

This is it then. I failed. In a few seconds, I'll be in Kog Prime's clutches again.

Thirteen counts down from ten. At 'three,' I power-down my koganzug. The biomechs wick away, pulled into the nodes installed all over my body, exposing puckered scars with the glint of steel in the middle of each. My Devil's mask falls from my face.

The stone floor feels cold against my naked body. My ribs and wrist throb with pain. Blood spills between my fingers from the wound in my side. With the armour gone, I'm nothing but a man made from bolts and matchsticks, easy to snap into pieces.

With the armour gone, I'm nothing but a man made from bolts and matchsticks, easy to snap into pieces.

You have powered-down, Thirteen declares.

Manny laughs loudly. He drops Wilhelm and walks over to me, squats so we're face to face. Picks up my plague blade and uses the tip to lift my chin.

"You're really this pretty? Look at those eyelashes! I thought it was a mask." He brandishes his claws, like he's going to stroke my face, about to start one of his games.

"Hold," Bann orders, voice devoid of emotion.

"But-" Manny whines.

"Touch him and I'll put the plague in you."

Manny glares at Bann, but he's as scared as he is angry.

"Watch this one while I carry out our orders," Bann

says, indicating me.

Manny stands, folds his arms across his chest and grumbles. Bann snatches my dagger out of Manny's hand and tosses it out of everyone's reach. He stares Manny down with that falsely smiling mask, daring him to protest again. Manny backs down.

Bann goes to Wilhelm. The scientist situates himself on his knees, but then he slowly pulls the strap of his satchel over his head. He tosses the satchel in my direction and looks me in the eye.

The letter in his satchel for his daughter...

I struggle to reach for it, but Manny knocks me down. Bann levels his sword with Wilhelm's neck and pulls back, ready for the final swing. Wilhelm holds my gaze, and all I can do is nod.

Yes, if I survive this, I'll deliver your letter.

After I nod, Wilhelm trains his eyes straight ahead, the blue of his irises glistening.

I close my eyes. I don't want to see it. I can't bear to see the results of my failure.

I hear Bann's blade cut through flesh, the thud of a

head, and the crash of a body hitting the floor.

"Bastard," I murmur, but I'm the one who failed.

Manny clubs me across the head, sends me sprawling to the floor. I try to roll away, but he kicks and catches me in the shoulder. Something pops and my arm flails, dislocated—the same arm with the broken wrist. Manny comes after me, intent on getting his claws into me.

"Manny," Bann says. His quiet voice cuts through the ruckus. Manny freezes.

Bann cleans his blade with his hand, the biomechs scrubbing the metal clean. He meticulously wipes the three holes at the tip and the etched designs. Lady Justice looks blindly on.

"Just let me kill him. You already got to kill the wench," Manny complains.

"Those aren't our order, but if you want to kill him so bad, go ahead. See what happens." Bann cocks his head, the wolf mask silently smiling at Manny.

Manny takes a step back.

"No?" Bann continues. "Then take the scientist's

body to the rendezvous."

Manny gathers up Wilhelm's body and head, muttering curses under his breath. He makes a kick at me on his way out, and I curl up like an insect.

After Manny leaves, the room falls silent. All I can hear is my own staggered breathing. Bann kneels on one knee beside me, but I have my back to him. The sound of metal sliding on metal meets my ears, his sword being drawn. I look back at him. He leans the blade against his shoulder.

"Thanks for not handing me to Manny," I say.

Bann is quiet for a moment before he asks. "You don't want to survive this, do you? That's why you chose to power down over being reclaimed."

I push myself up off the floor with my one good arm. My ribs throb in protest, but I'm just one body of pain at this point. I can't even spare a thought for my nakedness. I gather myself into a kneeling position. I smile, one hand clasping my wounded side and the other arm hanging awkwardly.

"I wanted to see what it was like," I reply.

"Freedom?" he asks.

I laugh softly, bitterly. "No, making a choice for myself. No Vogt. No Kog Prime. No lies. No owing anyone anything. But wanting something is as scary as I thought."

Bann stands and lifts his sword. I guess he's going to kill me instead of following orders. That's nice of him. It's just too bad I won't be able to deliver Wilhelm's letter to his daughter.

The words to the song Manny was singing pop into my head. I sing.

> "Ribbons to a rope,
> Anchored to the weight of hope,
> Becomes like time..."

My voice cracks with pain and exhaustion, but the words come to me—come from somewhere lost but not gone.

> "Back and forth and back again,
> Like a loom weaves a ribbon.
> Then twine your ribbon to mine.
>
> One drop, then two.
> Met together, me and you..."

Bann pauses, holding his blade aloft, and waits until I finish.

After the song is done, I laugh softly, grimacing with pain. "It's funny. I know all the words but not who sang them to me."

I cock my head to look up at Bann. The details of his wolf's mask blur. Blood loss must be getting to me.

"You know before I joined the Devils when you told me to leave?" I say. "The truth is I refused to leave because I have nowhere to go. You see, I can't remember a time when I wasn't a monster."

Bann sighs and lowers his sword. He plunges the tip into the wood floor beside me then leans against it, bowing his head down to my level.

"You want a chance?" He says in my ear. "How about we play a game? I'll give you one chance to run. But if you take this chance, you'd better bury yourself where I can never get to you because I'll be hunting you, and when I catch you I'll toss you to Kog Prime. Because if I catch you, you didn't want it bad enough. If I catch you, that's you choosing the life of a Devil."

I slump, smiling foolishly but too faint to care. "A chance would be nice."

Bann stands and snorts derisively, wrenching his blade free. "You always were a fool, Leiden."

He brings the pommel down on my head and everything goes dark.

Part 2

Nine weeks after Bergverk.

The Dustlands of Giya

Chapter 10: Two Halves and a Hole

∞

My Dearest Papa,

Are you well? I hope so.

∞

Three weeks travel by foot from the Port of Rettung. Twenty nights and twenty-one days. Approximately 920 kilometres.

My hammer pings, driving a nail through the sand into the underlying saltstone. The blow reverberates through my arms. I work like I'm well, but the blow aches deep in my bones.

Prop-up tents billow in the wind. We—the other railroad workers and I—move and pitch them each morning, following the course of the railroad tracks.

Two Halves and a Hole

Makes a place to keep the desert heat out during the day and keep the heat in during the night. Not the sand though. Nothing can stop the sand. Our bodies are coated with it day and night. It crunches between my teeth as I work.

Wagons follow the tents. Wagons for food. Wagons for equipment. Wagons for… other needs.

The blazing afternoon sun seems to burn straight through my clothes. Granted, my long-sleeved shirt and trousers are a bit tattered to prove much protection. They're more for hiding the bandages wrapping my arms and waist. The nodes in my body where the biomechs are supposed to deploy are weeping something fierce, leaving my bandages yellow and stiff even though I change them every day. At least my red schal keeps the worst of the heat off my head and neck.

I shift Wilhelm's satchel from one shoulder to the other. I can't set it down—someone will snatch it before even a grain of sand can settle on it.

It's shattering hot. Thank the Lights Above the work day is almost done.

The sound of metal pounding metal rings above the tearing desert wind. Sand and salt dance across the dunes, spraying my face and sticking to the sweat that dries as quick as it beads. My body prickles with sweat and aches with small wounds crusted in salt.

When I first joined the railroad workers, I complained about having a wagon for sex workers but none for doctors. The other workers laughed like I'd made a good joke. Of course there are no doctors. The railroad runs parallel to the refugee trail. With so many willing to replace any sick or injured, why would the company bother with doctors?

In the weeks since Bergverk, the Vogt has gripped the Reichland by the throat, establishing the Vogt der Wahrheit Government and rooting out any remnants of the Coalition. The new government also gave the Neo-Arkists their head, looking the other way while the new Noah, Clara Neuseman, terrorises hollowberns and hollowbern sympathisers. The resulting refugees have flooded Giya, a constant stream of them treading the path that runs parallel to the very railroad tracks I work on.

I swing again. My sledge hammer pounds the top of a railroad spike. Sand covers the tracks.

It's wishful thinking if the Vogt believes a train track crossing the desert will last more than a few years. Then again, the Vogt needs only a few years to conquer Giya. It never was a cohesive country, and now the influx of refugees is destabilizing it more, just as the Vogt intended.

But it won't last—not here in the Dustlands. Once the Vogt gets control of Giya's main port, it won't need the rail anymore. At that point, the desert will be let alone again. That's how it is here—the lines on the map might change, but the Dustlands never do.

Home never changes. There's good and bad in that.

A train blows its horn, coming in on the completed track to drop off more supplies and workers.

Jobs aren't scarce in Giya, considering the many mercenary and slaver crews, but food is, especially in the Dustlands. Between the railroad crews and the refugees, anything within ten kilometres of the railroad that can be shot, caught, or bought is scarce as my facial hair. That's why the railroad workers get paid in meal tokens. Anyone with a token gets a meal; except, with no doctors, these tokens change hands more than the company dares keep track of.

Makes it easy for a person to stay hidden. Staying alive? Not so much.

I prop my hammer against my foot, stretch my lower back, and wipe my stinging eyes against the bandages wrapping my hands.

You stink, Thirteen says, his words clear in my mind.

I roll my eyes. "You don't have a nose."

My sensors are more sensitive than your olfactory organs.

"Which means nothing. I won't apologise for a number."

I'm merely concerned for the welfare of your fellow workers.

I scoff and grip my hammer, pointing it at the worker across from me. Sweat has completely saturated his shirt, showing muscle and paunch beneath. "Does he look like he cares?" I ask. I gesture at the worker collapsed in the dirt behind me, gasping for air. "What about him?"

Neither worker comments on my one-man conversation. We've worked in the same crew for nearly a month. They've grown used to my brand of crazy.

Don't take your mood out on me, Thirteen protests. *I'm just telling you what the numbers are telling me and they say you need a bath.* He turns sulky. *Besides, you are the one who turned traitor and put us in this mess.*

"Twelve," I mutter.

Twelve what?

"That's the twelfth time you've blamed me today."

It's still early. Don't worry, I'll get the count up: This is all your fault. Only a miracle let us wake up in that safe house after Bergverk; otherwise, we'd definitely be dead, and it totally, absolutely, and completely would be your fault!

If Thirteen could sit on the floor and wail, that's what he'd be doing right now.

After Bergverk, by some miracle, I woke up alone in a safe house in the mountains. My wounds had been bandaged, and I'd been left in possession of Wilhelm's satchel, which contained two letters, the totems I'd carved, my plague blade and Devil's mask, a box of immuno-korrectives to fend off blood rot, and, of all things, Perri's heirloom music box.

That was eight weeks ago, and, coincidentally, Thirteen has been throwing a eight-week long tantrum.

Ultimately, Thirteen's right—the moment I failed to protect Wilhelm was the moment I should have died. Even now, I'm waiting for Bann to show up and finish me off. I failed my mission, turned traitor, failed at that, and deserted the Vogt...

And Bann is not the forgiving type.

I move down the line and swing my hammer, pounding the next spike into the track and tie and rock. One of the nodes on my arm splits. Blood seeps into the bandage, the colour of mud.

In truth, it's not Bann that worries me the most right now—it's blood rot. Without the protection of my koganzug, my compromised immune system is more susceptible to blood rot than the average Lowly. Plus, it's been a little over a week since I ran out of korrectives. If I don't reach the Port of Rettung soon, I won't be reaching it at all.

Hey, Thirteen chimes, *do you think if I successfully convince you to turn yourself in and Kog Prime sees the recording in your archives, it'll agree to keep me functional?*

"And what? Kill me but transplant you?"

I was thinking more like they would incarcerate you for the duration of your lifespan, but whatever works.

"Huh. Thanks," I scoff.

Thirteen gives a sigh that I equate with a shrug. *Better living than dead.*

"Not always," I say, more to myself than Thirteen. My hammer pounds metal, jarring my bones. "But I guess someone living by the numbers wouldn't understand that."

Thirteen doesn't reply. Either he's more sensitive than I give him credit for or he's confused. I can hope for the former, but I expect the latter. Either way, I'm thankful he stopped talking.

The train comes in, steam hissing from its engine. Workers shout over the noise and a bustle begins. People jump onto the train to check equipment or head up track. New crewmen jump down.

I take a wheel barrow to the ballast pile, but instead of loading up, I park it to the side and hike to the top of the pile with my shovel. Gets me to a better vantage point.

Thirteen doesn't say anything, but I know he's sorting through all the faces, searching for anyone we don't want to see. A few weeks before, we had to keep low when some Vogt officers came in on the train and transferred to autos.

Leviatan, do children normally come in on the train? Thirteen asks.

"Sometimes. They might be the children of one of the workers."

And if they cover their faces and avoid contact with anyone, that's because they want to surprise their parents, correct?

"Where?" I ask, alarmed.

Second car.

I spot the kids Thirteen noticed. They duck low between the equipment being offloaded and stay out of sight of the workers, heading into the maze of crates on the far side of the loading bay. They're covered head to toe. The wind pulls off the schal of the bigger of the two, revealing a pale face with brown hair pulled up in a top bun. The kid tugs the schal back on, glancing around furtively for witnesses.

If they held a sign over their heads that read, "We don't belong here," it couldn't have been more obvious.

"Judging by how they're covered, they might be hollowberns fleeing the genocide," I offer. "The Port of Rettung has become a haven for hollowberns fleeing the Reichland."

Company, Thirteen says.

I catch sight of them just as Thirteen says it. Three men step off the third car. Their attention is trained on the two kids sneaking away from the offloading bay.

The men quickly strip off their casual clothes, revealing skin-tight combat suits underneath. They pull black masks over their heads and faces.

I groan. Shattering anzug users. Their suits are nothing compared to my koganzug, just the slip-on-slip-off type and not anatomically integrated. They only slightly improve the user's strength and stealth, but they still can be a pain in the ass to fight, especially in the condition I'm in.

One man motions for the other two to go in opposite directions and circle around the maze of crates the kids are passing through. He'll go down the middle.

It's a pincer attack. Those kids are screwed.

I take a step in the direction of the loading bay, gripping my shovel tightly.

Don't do it, Thirteen warns. *We have our own problems.*

"I can handle them," I reply.

So what? You handle them; someone reports you; then Captain Bann finds us. We both die. The end.

"He's not my captain anymore."

Which is why he wants to kill us.

"I can at least warn them."

Yeah, because that will be helpful, Thirteen replies sarcastically. He's made great progress with sarcasm lately.

We'll walk up and say, 'Hi! Three mercenaries in high-tech combat suits are after you. Good luck!' Not to mention, with the way the kids are behaving, they already know they're being followed.

"Then what should I do?" I ask in aggravation.

Nothing. Do nothing. If that's too hard for you, then let's go back to the Vogt. Either way, you die, but if you go back, then I might get to live.

My knuckles ache with the death grip I have on my shovel. The two kids are almost through the maze of crates at the loading bay. The far end opens up to the refugee trail. If they make it that far, they could blend in with the refugees, but the anzug users are already closing in. The kids are running headlong into an ambush.

A high-pitched keen pierces the air. Workers near

the train engine shout at each other, jumping off the car.

'What-'

Down. Thirteen says it in a tone that broaches no argument.

I drop to a crouch just as the engine car explodes. The concussion knocks me off the ballast pile, and I roll down the gravel, ears ringing. I try to stand, but my balance is off, and I topple over. I roll onto my back and stare at the black clouds of smoke billowing into the dust-filled sky. The wind snatches the clouds away, leaving only a grey haze behind.

A high-pitched keen rings in my ears, accompanied by a fierce headache. My eyes throb, but the pain goes deeper than that. It's piercing.

I crush Wilhelm's satchel to my chest, knocked senseless but somehow desperate to protect it.

In it, there's the letter written by Wilhelm's daughter. I've read it so many times that it is tearing at the folds.

There's also Wilhelm's letter to her, still sealed and waiting for his daughter's hand to receive it.

Two Halves and a Hole

There are my totems: a red schal, an old auto, a wooden soldier and a toy elephant, a lamp, a pendent, and now a music box…

My past, present, and future…

These things are me. They are everything I am. They are the most important.

I know I'm not thinking straight—I know my brain was addled by the explosion—but all I can think is to protect this satchel. My body is a hollow shell; it's the satchel that carries my soul.

High-pitched keening rings in my ears and a nightmarish headache tears through my mind, splintering my thoughts.

My head is an old house with wind shrieking in the eaves. My heart is a backdoor slamming against my ribs, pulsing in my head.

My memories are the dust on the floor.

Chapter 11: Remember

∞

Papa, since you left, I've often thought of my childhood. Specifically, the day it ended.

∞

A dream unfolds, a hallucination, and I watch and live it at the same time. It's hard to distinguish which thoughts come from my child-self living the dream and which come from me in hindsight.

It doesn't matter though. Both are me, and both lead to—and are the result of—what I chose to become.

Chapter 12: Freude

Nine years ago.

Freude looked striking in his grey-blue uniform, his red schal wrapped around his neck and shoulders like a cloak. Mum had made the schal for him when he'd turned twelve, a traditional come-of-age gift. She'd stayed up late for weeks stitching the delicate embroidery.

Freude's newly shorn hair glinted like copper in the brilliant desert sun. He'd cut his Dustlander braids himself. He'd look handsome if it weren't for his injuries from last night's festival—stitches on his right eyebrow, a split lip, and bandaged knuckles. All four of us brothers had a few trophies on display and we wore them proudly despite Mum's glares.

Freude pulled on his military cap. The emblem of the Vogt Faction, the two-headed dragon, emblazoned his hat. His schal hid the same symbol on his right sleeve and the lapels of his jacket. The uniform had come by post, delivered by one of the Vogt's messengers. They said Freude should already be wearing it when he reported.

He, Ehren, and Keim all had Mum's red hair. Not me. I didn't have Da's hair neither even though the rest of me looked like a younger version of him. Same long face and strong nose. Same big eyes the colour of gold. But I guess I got my mum's long temper instead of his short one.

I asked Mum why my hair was different from the rest of our family's. She teased me, saying that the Goddess kissed me at birth and infused my hair with the light of her beloved sister moon. That's why my hair shimmered with blue iridescence. I asked Mum if the Goddess kissed her too so her haired turned red like the scamp moon.

She shook her head and replied with a sad smile, "No, she spat on me."

Guess she spat on my brothers too then. Serves them right.

Da—tall, broad, and swarthy—stood off to the side from the rest of us and grumbled about the Vogt's recruiting methods. Seems he always placed himself off to the side when it came to his family.

"Shattering slavery, that's what it is," Da muttered, jerking savagely on his schal like he'd wrapped his neck too tightly with it. Mum shushed him, glancing at me and Keim, but it wasn't anything we hadn't heard before.

As the civil war in the Reichland dragged on, it demanded new blood to sustain it, and those Reichlanders found ways to get it. All it took was a few thousand marcs and Giya's city-lords had come running.

Some of Giya's city-lords worked through slavers, allowing them to run rampant in their territories, kidnapping or raiding, and other city-lords sold their citizens outright. Our city-lords, the self-proclaimed "Lord of the Desert," decided to levy a draft. We had to pick who'd be sold from among us.

Freude though, he chose to enlist.

The military auto arrived, one of the newly designed cargo haulers with a steel frame, engine and cab in front and a big canvas-covered bed for cargo or people in back.

Keim was drawn to it like a magnet. He might be only thirteen, but he was already devoted to reengineering and relics. With the discovery of the steel oxidization method, the Vogt had been turning out new products en masse. No more wood auto frames or porcelain knives. No more crossbows neither. No matter, Keim loved it all.

The cargo hauler roared up to our station and stopped. The driver leaned out, bowler cap pulled low over his eyes, and spat strauch chew at our feet.

"This gods-forsaken place Baumfeld?" he asked.

Da shoved his hands in his pockets and straightened his back. "Might be," he growled.

"You the Talson family?"

"Who's asking?"

"The Vogt," the man said and spat again.

The Vogt. That's all he needed to say. Da looked like he had a lot more to say, but Mum put a hand on his shoulder.

Freude set down his duffel bag to say his farewells. He hugged Mum, and she handed him a bag of her *vanillekipferl* cookies. He kissed her on the cheek and put the bag in his duffel. When he straightened, Mum placed a hand on his face, tears in her eyes.

Seeing Mum, I began to cry too. I crouched down and put my head against my knees so he couldn't see. I was too grown for this. Nearly nine years old was too old to be crying.

Freude knelt in front of me. I peeked at him from my knees. He unwrapped his schal and held the bundle of red fabric in front of me, Mum's careful embroidery crumpled in on itself in his hand. "I won't be needing this. You take it."

I stared at the needlepoint spirals and waves, one of

the great sandstorms stitched into fabric.

"You're about all grown now, aren't you?" Freude asked, winking.

I took a deep breath, rubbed my sleeve over my face, and nodded. "Okay."

He wrapped it around my shoulders, pulled it over my iridescent hair to be a headscarf. It smelled like home, like strauch trees, incense, and dust.

"Red for luck," he said, smirking. Then he jerked the schal down over my face and chuckled. I grumbled, tugging it back into place.

Freude stood, took a few steps back, and gazed at us together. Mum fidgeted with her healer pendant. Da put an arm around her waist, stilling her, and a hand on Keim's shoulder. Ehren stood a little distance away, feeling too mature to betray emotion but too upset to look up from his shoes.

Except for Mum, Ehren loved Freude best. Ehren had always done as Freude did and gone where Freude went, until now.

Now, Ehren would not look up as Freude shouldered

his bag and smiled. He would not look up as Freude turned and walked away from him, away from us, and climbed into the back of the hauler.

Ehren would not see Freude again.

Neither would we.

∞

A year later, a knock sounded at the front door. From my bedroom, I pressed my face against the slats of my window to see who it was, but sand scummed up the glass. I couldn't see the front door from there anyway, but a shadow milled about outside the gate. It looked like an animal with four long legs and a whip-like tail, a messenger mount.

Not a neighbour then.

Keim and Ehren listened to the radio in the living room, procrastinating evening chores. The local newsman murmured over the wrinkle of static. I could hear the voice but not the words. Mum rolled *vanillekipferl* cookies in the kitchen. Da worked on the harvester in back.

I couldn't see the messenger due to the dugout, a

tunnel that protected visitors from the wind and sand until we could get to the door. The low-ceiling and narrow walls of the dugout made for a tight fit though. I probably wouldn't be able to stand upright in it next year. One reason we always used the backdoor.

Another knock.

I sat back down at my desk. Ehren would get the door as soon as me or Keim made a go of it. I wanted to stay out of it this time so I focused on my comic page. A Sky Saint punched a scribbled mass of leaden darkness with a fist three times too large, his face flawlessly human. I added a circle at the top of the page and wrote "Ka-Bam" in the jagged, bold font I'd seen in the books the Arkist missionaries handed out.

A lot of people liked those books. Freude loved them. Mum didn't.

Knocks sounded again. Did they know we were home?

"Can someone get that?" Mum called from the kitchen.

I leaned out from my desk to get a clear view of the

living room. To see what my brothers would do.

"I will," Keim yelled, jumping up from the couch in the living room.

Ehren cut in front of Keim. "Too slow."

"No fair," Keim whined. "I'm telling Ma."

Ehren poked Keim in the head with his index finger. "Tell her what? That I answered the door because you took forever to get to it? Don't be stupid." He poked Keim's head again, shoving it to the side.

"Stop it! That hurt."

"'Stop it,'" Ehren mocked, smirking.

Keim's eyes welled up, and he ran toward the kitchen. "Mum!"

"I didn't do anything!" Ehren called after him.

Knocking, this time longer and louder, interrupted his defence.

Whoever waited on the other side of the door had probably heard the argument. Curious about the person who'd bothered to knock so many times, I left my room and took the long way around, avoiding Ehren, which took me past the kitchen. I could hear Keim sniffling at the table. Da had come in from the back. He and Mum were talking as I passed the kitchen door, their voices rising as their conversation headed toward an argument.

"Just ask Ehren about what he's interested in once in a while," Da said.

"I ask him all the time," Mum answered.

"But you always bring up Freude. Stop comparing him to Freude. He's his own person."

"What's wrong with bringing up Freude? He worships Freude."

"But he's not Freude."

"I know he's not Freude."

"I know, but sometimes you make him feel like that's a bad thing."

I heard Mum's footsteps head my way.

"Someone is at the door," she said, ending the conversation.

Ehren wrenched open the front door before Mum reached it. I followed behind, wondering who'd waited at the door so long.

A man in a blue uniform with the Vogt's symbol

emblazoned on the sleeve stood in our dugout. Fine grains of sand rippled down the steps behind him. Upon seeing him, Ehren stood taller and squared his shoulders.

"Letter for the Talson household."

"I'll take it," Ehren intoned, pitching his voice lower.

Curious, I sidled over to Ehren to watch.

The officer shrugged and handed Ehren a ledger. Ehren signed, but as he returned the ledger and pen and reached for the letter, Mum snatched it. Ehren scowled then retreated to the living room to sulk—away from us but not so far away he couldn't hear.

The officer didn't wait to see her open it, just turned and trotted down the lane to where his mount pawed at the dirt with its three-toed feet. I shut the door after him.

Mum's face lit up in the way only a letter from Freude could do. She slid a kitchen knife down the length of the envelope. We waited quietly while Mum opened it. She unfolded the page. Her eyes scanned it.

Freude

We waited while Mum opened it. She slit the envelope and unfolded the page. Her eyes scanned it.

Then they scanned it again.

As she scanned it a third time, all the colour drained from her face. Even her eyes seemed to fade. Her lips turned white, but they remained frozen in a smile. Then I realised she wasn't breathing.

"Mum," I said softly.

Nothing.

"Mum!"

She shook herself suddenly and looked at us—Keim and Ehren on the couch, Da at the backdoor, me near the hall. Her smile widened like shattered earth, a fissure cut into stone.

She set the letter aside. "Dinner will be ready soon. Don't forget to wash."

Then she walked back into the kitchen. The two-way door swung back and forth. A few seconds later, pans clattered and crockery shattered, and a broken, half-baked *vanillekipferl* cookie slid through the swinging door.

Da frowned and picked up the letter. Read it. Bowed his head.

"Da?" Ehren asked. His voice squeaked.

Da lifted his face. Grief lined his dark features. All Da said was, "He's dead."

"Who?" I asked, confused.

Ehren started from his seat, but couldn't move farther. We just stared at Da, and Da stared back. He opened his mouth. Closed it again. Shook his head.

I took the page from him, and tried to read the notice aloud, tried to do what we were all waiting for, but no one had the power to do—to voice the disaster. But I was only almost ten, and I stumbled over some of the words.

"Un-for-"—I pronounced slowly—"Un-for--"

"Just shut up," Ehren snarled. "You sound like a clinking idiot. Just shut up."

I lowered the paper. Ehren stood with his fists clenched at his sides. His whole body trembled. Tears coursed down his face. The tapping of Mum's knife in the kitchen filled the silence.

Freude

"You're all shattering idiots. Gods damn you all. I hate this family." Then Ehren ran out the backdoor.

Keim began to cry. Da sat on the couch and pulled him into his lap even though he was nearly fourteen. But Keim let him. Just buried his face in Da's shoulder and sobbed.

I still clutched the paper. "Da, what happened to Freude?"

Da shook his head at me.

"What happened to Freude?"

He looked away.

"Da," I kept calling. "Da…"

But I no longer existed to my father. He could not acknowledge me without acknowledging my question, and if he acknowledged my question, he had to acknowledge the answer.

Freude had died in an "unfortunate incident." His remains were not suitable for transport or for proper burial. He had no personal effects. Condolences.

Mum never baked *vanillekipferl* cookies again.

Chapter 13: Burned

∞

On the day my childhood ended, a
hollowbern man was beaten in the street
in front of us. Do you remember?

∞

I emerge from the memory feeling breathless and lay panting at the bottom of the ballast pile. Did the train explosion knock me out? How long have I been laying here?

The dream felt long, long and exhausting, but at least my headache is fading.

Cover. Debris, Thirteen says in that same firm tone.

Debris? Thirteen's order confuses me, but I curl into a ball anyway, covering my head with my arms.

Burned

Chunks of metal and stone fall around me, the remains of the engine car, tracks, and saltstone foundation. People scream nearby.

That's when I realise it has only been seconds. To go from a kid living in a small town to a grown man dodging falling debris—the disorientation leaves me feeling wretched. Was that a dream? A hallucination? Or was it a memory? Could that have been me? Was that my family?

Leviatan, Thirteen yells sharply, w*hat are you doing? Now is not the time to contemplate the impracticality of bipedal mobility.*

"What?" I ask, startled.

Stop staring at your feet and move! Now would be the best opportunity to extricate ourselves from our current predicament and to find a new one.

He's right. Now isn't the time to sort my thoughts. The dust is settling. Soon, this place will be swarming with people trying to help the injured and collect the dead. There will also be company security investigating the bombing, and Vogt officers will be inbound.

I get to my feet and glance at the tracks. What I see stuns me. It wasn't just the engine car that exploded. The entire length of the train did, leaving the tracks underneath mangled.

How long was the train? A kilometre? Two? Several months of work erased in a moment. This was no small operation. Who had the manpower, skills, and pockets to fund something like this?

The Vogt had grown stronger but so had its enemies. Serves them right.

Whoever it was, they burned me good. Security will be tight after this.

As the thought occurs, Thirteen delivers the news. *Vogt agents will be inbound to investigate the bombing. I believe we've overstayed our welcome.*

Of course. I take a shard of saltstone, grit my teeth, and bash it on my head.

I knew it, Thirteen simpers. *It was only a matter of time before you went mad.*

A matter of time? I wonder. I've had voices in my head for years. Instead, I say, "The blood will obscure my face. Make it harder for anyone to get a bead on me."

You mean literally, don't you? I would like it if you mean that literally. Let's not die getting shot in the back and turned in for a bounty.

I don't bother to reply.

The head wound bleeds a lot, but it looks worse than it is. While everyone else seeks out friends or family, I pass through the tents and out toward the edge of camp.

At the edge of camp, I take out my food token. I'd hoped this gig and the token would take me all the way to Rettung, but I guess it'll have to take someone else instead. I chuck the token over the tops of the tents as hard as I can. In all this sweat, blood, and sand, maybe it'll bring some poor sod a bit of luck.

Chapter 14: The Bastard

∞

You didn't want me to see how ugly the world
can be and tried to cover my eyes, but I
wouldn't let you

∞

The shadows grow long with the evening. The bombing was well-timed. The culprits can easily disappear into the approaching darkness.

I round the outside of the railroad camp and head through a ravine. The refugee trail is on the other side. The strauch trees snatch at my clothes and claw at my face. I tie Freude's schal around Wilhelm's satchel so it doesn't clatter.

'Red for luck,' my brother said in my dream. I can

only hope I've been stockpiling luck all these years.

Stop! Thirteen shouts.

I stop so hard I nearly fall on my arse. "What now?"

Thirteen shushes me. *Someone is coming this way.*

I crouch in the strauch trees, listening. In truth, it's Thirteen listening for me. My ears are more useful used by him—even in his passive mode—than by me. Not only that, but comparing the results against his archive data provides him with much higher and more accurate discernment.

An adult. By the stride and vocalizations, likely a male.

A culprit, perhaps? Supposedly the enemy of my enemy is a friend, but after being a Devil for five years, I've learned that sometimes they're all enemies.

I unclip a pocketknife from the waistband of my trousers. Even though I have my plague blade strapped to the inside of my shoulder under my shirt, stabbing someone with it would definitely leave a trail for Bann. I keep the pocketknife low, shielding the blade from the setting sun, and still my breathing to listen.

A man appears from the trees not a meter away, his head and shoulders looming above the trees and his back turned. He's short and muscled with multi-pigmented skin, a patch of brown here and a touch of green there—a Lowly but not a hollowbern.

He looks nervous, twitchy, like he's on the run.

I shift for a better view, and a twig snaps under my heel. Damn.

The man jumps like he's been booted in the rear, and without a backward glance, he bolts through the trees in the opposite direction.

Did he see us? Thirteen asks.

"How would I know? That's something you're supposed to figure out," I snap, shoving my knife in my bag and running after the man.

If he saw us, do you think he's seen our bounty listing, too? He's going to report us. You should deploy your koganzug and report to Kog Prime first. I'm sure we'll get a more lenient punishment that way.

"I'm going to deliver that letter if it kills us so shut your gods-damned trap," I snarl, charging through the trees.

My trap is your trap, he retorts.

Whether this clinker recognised us or not, I'm going to find out just for the satisfaction of contradicting Thirteen. I growl a retort as I dodge around trees, hot on the stranger's tail.

I know. I know, Thirteen says. *'Shove off.'*

The stranger takes a narrow animal track into the ravine I just came from, trying to lose me. My bones ache with each bound. Dry air tears at my throat. It takes all I have just to keep the man in sight.

We reach a fork and the man goes one way while I go the other. Just as I reach the end of mine, the man passes the exit. I launch at him and knock us both into the sand. Moving quickly, I pin him, a knee in his back and arms leveraged painfully.

I'm silently thankful I remembered how to move. Without my koganzug, I wasn't certain what I'd recall. Thank the Lights Above for muscle memory.

"Get off me, ya filth!" The man's city cant jumbles his Common. His jaw swings open and closed like it's unhinged, and his tongue shoves out some syllables and swallows others.

I wrench his arms. "Who are you? What are you doing out here?"

"What?" he growls. I wrench his arms again and shove his face into the sand. "Lights Above, lay off! I seen it out there, went asking if they need help."

"Seen what?" I ask, twisting a finger.

"Gods save me, you'll rip it off," he shouts. "The wagon. The wagon!"

I twist harder.

"Fine," he squeals. "I gone seen what I could steal. Sol'ary wags is easy picks."

A solitary wagon? I release his hand. "And what did you find?"

"They're dead," he replies, voice quiet.

So he was robbing corpses.

'Maybe those anzug users weren't after the kids,' I subvocalize to Thirteen. 'Could they have attacked this wagon, or even the train?'

Possibly.

I speak to the man on the ground. "Did you see anyone else? Were there any witnesses?"

He hesitates, swallows hard. "No, they're all dead."

A shudder runs through the man. Fear cords the tendons of his neck like a noose, and panic rims his eyes.

"Thirteen?" I murmur.

He seems to be telling the truth. At least, the statements he has given are true, though possibly not the whole truth. That's not something I can ascertain by observation.

I release the man and step back.

The man lurches to his feet and stumbles away. He grumbles and rolls his shoulders as he turns around, and I finally see his face. A scar spans it from hairline to jaw, turning one eye milky and twisting his lips. He spits to the side and wipes sand from his cheek.

"Fract'ed little clinker," he snarls. "Piece of work, ain't ya?"

I fake a lunge at him, and the man flinches. Faintly amused, I allow a cold smile to part my lips.

The man snorts, gives me the knock, and walks away.

I let him go. He's given me news of somewhere else I need to be.

∞

I smell the destruction before I see it, the stench of burning flesh and blood. Wild urvogels swoop down to scavenge the remains, snake-like heads craned and silver eyes fixed on the clearing ahead of me. A long-toothed rat grunts in the brush to my left, drawn by the blood. Its massive jaws click in anticipation.

I break through the clearing and surprise the urvogels. They leap into the air screaming and leave dingy, rust-red feathers to drift into the dirt. Their raucous cries alert the rat. It halts in the trees, blinking blindly, nose in the air and twitching. It smells death and wants to make a meal of it, but it also smells me. It'll wait.

A middle-aged man with skin black as ebony lies on the ground facedown. A woman, probably his wife, rests nearby. Both had clawed hands but were rich enough to have them resculpted.

The wagon is a flatbed, Thirteen observes.

A flatbed. Good for transporting cargo. So, they're probably Reichlander merchants. The Dustlands has a way of inverting the hierarchy. Out here, the rich suffer most. They're the low-hanging fruit.

Blood clots the sand around the man and woman, but the blood isn't all theirs. The carcass of a half-butchered draft herp contributes most to the mess. Its tail and most of its belly are gone, and swarms of bloodflies crawl over the scales of its back and reptilian head. The wagon huddles behind the carnage like a frightened beastie—canvas stripped, wheels shattered, empty and broken.

I imagine the scar-faced man searching the wagon and frisking the corpses. My fists clench. He didn't kill them, but still... Bastard.

The anxiety I've felt since spotting the anzug users increases, turns my stomach. There's nothing here that tells me what I need to know. Namely, are those anzug users after me?

I kick a rock in frustration. It skitters past the bodies. I'm about to leave when the silver-haired man's hand twitches. I can hardly believe it, but the man's hand twitches again. I crouch beside him and turn him over.

The stench of burned flesh fills my nose. My stomach heaves. Peeling white and grey skin covers the man's chest. I can see blackened bone and cauterized blood vessels. The man is dead, but his body hasn't realised it yet.

Thirteen identifies the wound. *Ion hand canon blast.*

Ion hand canon? Whoever it was must be well-funded.

I touch the man's shoulder. "Sir, can you hear me?"

The man's lips move, but no words reach me. I lean my head down, my ear brushing the man's lips.

"Daughter," he whispers.

Daughter? Slavers then, and they took his daughter for the brothels. Even if it was the anzug users, it means they're not after me.

"Daughter," the man whispers again, his voice grating. He weakly raises a hand and points to the east.

I unsling my canteen. "How long?" I ask Thirteen.

The woman hasn't been dead long, maybe two hours?

"If the slavers left on foot, they might be only ten kilometres away. If they took an auto, they'll be much farther, but either way…"

I trail off. Either way, what?

Either way, I already know what will happen. I won't save his daughter even when I can. I glimpse a node peeking from beneath my sleeve. I scowl and tug the sleeve down.

Leviatan-

"You don't need to say it, Thirteen," I interrupt. "You've said it enough."

I kneel beside the dying man. "Sorry," I murmur. "I'm so sorry."

The man groans and pinches his eyes shut. A tear trickles down his cheek, cutting a clean track in the dust. I rinse his face and pour a little water into his mouth. He coughs, spitting most of it out.

"Daughter," he says again as he slips into a coma.

He dies a few minutes later.

I walk away. Who's the bastard now?

Chapter 15: Embers and Ash

∞

*You didn't want me to lose my
innocence, but witnessing cruelty is not
the end of innocence. It allows
innocence to grow into its power.*

∞

That night, I warm my too-thin limbs beside my fire, the yellow flames consuming sand and wood together. I tug my blanket over my shoulders and try to fend off the chill, but the warmth can't go deep enough. Not when the chill is caused by fever.

Shivering, I dig in Wilhelm's satchel and pull out the pages the scientist's daughter wrote to her father.

She wrote the letter in a Reichlander local dialect

with only a smattering of Manual. Surprising since her father spoke to me in fluent Manual, but that may have been due to his profession.

I like her use of dialect. There's a wholesomeness to it, a feeling of home.

I've read her words so many times that the words have begun to fade at the folds, but no matter how I try, I can't seem to memorise them. It's as if I read her words anew each time; I see her thoughts in new ways.

We're having a conversation, she and me, somehow through this letter.

I stare at the flames. Will I live long enough to deliver her father's letter, or will I fail in that, too? Bann and the Vogt can't be far behind.

"Das Vogt der Wahrheit," I enunciate in precise Manual.

It means, The Steward of Truth. That is the name of the new government the Vogt established after the massacre at Bergverk. The name, even just the thought of it, tastes of bile to me, but that is the only life I've ever known simply because I could never remember anything else.

"Thirteen, is there a town in the Dustlands called Baumfeld?" I ask, a knot tightening in my stomach.

Yes, there is. It is a farming community focused almost entirely on strauch production.

"Was there a family called Talson that lived there?"

I do not have access to Giya citizenship archives. However, I do have the Dustlands census conducted ten years ago for military recruitment purposes. It appears there was a Talson family in residence of Baumfeld at that time: a male-female Lowly pair with four male Lowly offspring.

My breath catches, frozen in my chest. "What are their names?"

Oldest to youngest: Mal Talson, Ella Talson, Freude Talson, Ehren Talson, Keim Talson, and Leiden Talson...

Hey, that's you!

The names land like gut punches, forcing the stuck air out of my lungs.

How did you know that?

"I…" I take a deep breath, trying to ease the knot in my stomach, but it's not working. "I… remembered."

Oh.

That's all Thirteen says in reply to my revelation. I don't know what to think so it's no surprise he doesn't know what to say. We sit quietly, the crackling of the fire filling our silence.

Leviatan, Thirteen says, breaking the silence, *is it hard to be human?*

A branch in the fire splits and a streamer of smoke squirms up from between the pieces.

"Is this a survey question?"

I… he says, actually sounding hesitant. *I suppose it is.*

Do I dare answer Thirteen's question? When the Vogt first made me into a weapon, I thought I owed them for saving my life. I didn't know Bann saved me only to kill me slowly. If he'd told me the truth—if he'd quit making up stories about what his job was like and told me the truth of it—I never would have chosen that life.

Kog Prime stripped away my memories, but Bann stripped away my humanity.

I prod the embers with a stick. Smoke curls into the cool night like ribbons and carries the scent of charred strauch tree sap. It reminds me of home, of the strauch tree harvest and the pungent smoke of strauch bark. To me, it's also the scent of children's toys and vanillekipferl cookies, of a canary yellow kitchen and musty couches that billow dust. It's the scent of the home my mother raised me in—the home I left in another life.

Sometimes, when I was a Devil, I saw that home in my dreams and wish I could stay there, find that place and never leave, find a place where no one ever leaves.

But such a place doesn't exist. It never did.

I remember now. My home was a lie, a rope neatly bound in slipknots—one good tug unravelled it all.

Branches pop like gunshots, the hot sap bursting. Sparks explode into the air. I prop my chin on my hand, a dusting of stubble scraping across my knuckles. A headache knocks at the back of my head.

"Wilhelm's daughter wrote that not turning away was all she had to offer," I murmur, massaging my temples, "but what difference does that make? It's still doing nothing."

Leviatan? Thirteen asks, confused.

I sigh and flick the stick into the fire. It catches and bursts into flame. Then, just as suddenly, it turns to embers and ash.

"Yes," I reply, lying down to sleep. "It's very hard to be human."

My head throbs and there's a ringing in my ears as I go to bed.

Chapter 16: Ehren

Seven years and eleven months ago.

I walked through the backdoor wrapping a gauze bandage around my forearm. My alpha urvogel had clawed me just above the protective leather gloves when I tried collecting her single measly egg. I'd even set bait outside the roost to distract her. So much for that! That feather-brained turd had far too much intelligence for a lizard.

Sweat prickled my scalp, ran along the rows between my braids, and slipped down my neck to soak into Freude's schal and my shirt. Both garments clung to my skin, sticky and stinking.

It was one of those days—a 'Hell day' my da called

it—when nothing and no one could handle any more heat. I tried to cool off in the crick, but the heat just got passed around—me to the crick and the crick to the sand, the sand to the house and the house back to me—round and round til there was no escaping the misery.

In the kitchen, Ehren stood with his back to me. His schal hung around his shoulders, drenched in sweat like mine. He levelled a flathead shovel at a mud skink curled in the corner. Mum sat at the kitchen table, rigidly upright with her hands clasped around a clay mug with a chipped lip. Steam curled off the hot tea.

Hot tea on a day like this?

She stared straight ahead, eyes vacant. I stood a few feet from her. Blood seeped through my gauze bandage, the deep red stain stark on the fabric, but she just sat and stared with sweat trickling down her temples and steam curling up from between her hands.

A bad day then.

Da had stayed in back to collect milk from our spined bovine and finish up the morning chores. I'd taken to helping him in the mornings and evenings, especially with the urvogels. He'd said ten isn't too young to do a grown up's work.

Besides, I was all the help he had. Keim studied in his room and worked at the market in his off time, mostly to stay away from Ehren. Ehren stayed in his room, writing. Writing and thinking. Thinking and writing. What he did with all those words, I never knew. And Mum...

Mum had been a physician once, back in the Reichland before the civil war. But now, she spent most of her time in bed or staring out the kitchen window toward the road.

That left me to help Da. I must've been doing well too because Da had started giving me more jobs while he went into town. I couldn't do them as quick as he or Ehren might—finished real late some nights—but I got it done.

"Die," Ehren hissed.

He stabbed the shovel at the skink, but the hard corners of the scoop caught the wall. The beastie wriggled beneath the shovel and shot past Ehren's feet.

Those little legs could move quick.

I dove to the floor and scooped it up just as Ehren turned around with the shovel.

His red hair clung to his forehead, damp with sweat. Heat flushed his cheeks. He glared at me, pale lavender eyes turned black with shadow, and smiled with all his teeth. Me and Keim knew that expression well—it threatened violence.

He brandished the shovel at me. "Put it down!"

The lizard squirmed in my hands. Its sinuous tail curled around my good forearm. It'd probably come in trying to escape the heat. Mum used to like them, let them hunt in her garden for pests.

I looked at her for help, but she sat in the exact same position as before, her eyes hooked on the road. If it weren't for Ehren, I'd wonder if I were there at all.

"Put it down," Ehren growled.

I glanced past Ehren to the backdoor, hoping Da might come through it. "It's not hurting anyone. Let me put it outside."

"I want to kill it."

"But you don't need to."

"But I want to!"

I stepped back toward the living room, the creature's padded feet clinging to my hand. My eyes locked with Ehren's for a moment. Ehren's narrowed, his hands tightening on the shovel. His lip shivered with a nervous twitch.

The twitch was what I'd been waiting for. I ducked and rolled at the same time Ehren swung the shovel at me. The metal clanged against the floorboards where I'd stood and splintered the wood. I banged into the kitchen table and lay sprawled for a moment, dizzy. Mum's mug of tea fell from the table, breaking neatly in two, and splashed me with scalding tea.

Mum stood up from the table. "What the devil are you boys doing!" she shouted.

Ehren swung at me again. I barely had enough time to curl around the beastie. The shovel thudded against my shoulder. The muscles bruised deeply, but I sealed my lips against a scream. I wouldn't give Ehren the satisfaction.

Ehren

Mum knelt on the floor, collecting the pieces of the mug and ignoring us. Freude had made the mug for her. For her, only those two broken pieces existed.

Ehren swung again, but this time I rolled beneath the swing and collided with his legs. He stumbled so I lunged for the backdoor, the skink clutched against my chest. The hinges groaned loudly as I wrenched it open.

Suddenly, the shovel clanged against the wall beside me, loud as a church bell, and the handle hit Mum's teapot on the counter. It shattered, exploded like a firecracker, but Mum didn't notice.

Ehren had made that for her.

I passed the threshold, jumped off the porch into the gravel, and kept running. The gravel crunched beneath my boots like grinding teeth, and the heat swallowed me whole.

My shoulder ached and the gauze bandage began to unwind, but I couldn't stop—too much adrenaline, too much fear, too much to run from—and the beastie scrabbled and hissed against my chest all the while.

∞

I came in late after releasing the skink down by the crick. The sun had set, but the scamp moon wasn't up yet. Just stars shone in the sky, since the sister moon had already set for the season. She wouldn't be up again until the turn of the year. No more moonlit harvests. No more eclipses in the day. Just a moonless hour before the scamp moon's rise and complete dark outside.

In the kitchen, shards of crockery still scattered the counter and floor. The shovel still lay beside it, and Mum's mug lay broken on the table with the tea dried on the floor.

A candle flickered on the table. The wax had overflowed the drip pan. Last year, Da had wanted to get the reengineered candles, the flameless kind, but Mum had refused—said the torchlamps were enough even though they have to be wound to work.

Mum had refused any changes since Freude. She'd have stopped me from growing if she could. Kept me in the same old clothes even though I'd grown at least ten centimetres since Freude left. My trousers hiked up something awful, but I still couldn't fit Keim's.

Maybe that's why she couldn't see me anymore? I'd changed too much—changed beyond her recognition.

The flame flickered, throwing shadows across the counters and table and striking reflections on the windows.

Funny how light inverts things, brings out the darkness of what's lit.

I rubbed my eyes with the heels of my hands. When I pulled them away, spots of light danced in my vision for a moment. I sighed as they faded. I felt wrung of emotion, sparse, like a skin stuffed with sticks and straw rather than bones and flesh.

I dragged myself through the kitchen into the living room. My boots clumped on the wood floor. I plopped down in front of the shoe rack, fumbled with laces, and wrestled my boots off. Then I shuffled down the hall toward my room in my socks. A big toe stuck through one and a heel stuck through the other.

Heat eased up through the floor, the house still passing it around after the scorching day. While outside, I'd sweated through my clothes, but the sun dried it. Now the stiffened fabric chaffed my skin. All I wanted was to strip to my drawers and crawl into bed.

A crash sounded from my room. My door was shut, but light beamed from beneath it. A thud on the door, and the light flashed as someone moved on the other side of it. A sense of dread crept into my belly. I twisted the knob and pushed it open. It creaked as it swung wide.

Ehren stood in the middle of my room with his back to me, one of Mum's paring knives in his hand. He'd wound my torchlamp, and it sat on the dresser beside Freude's schal, lighting the room in a steady yellow glow. Scraps of my drawings scattered the floor around him, depictions of the Holy Sky People.

We hadn't much paper to spare so I'd drawn multiple frames on every centimetre of paper I could get my hands on. I'd swiped old newspapers from Da, coloured over the articles about the civil war in the Reichland. The losses and victories made no difference to me. I'd drawn pictures of angels and demons, had scrawled over headline words like "war," and "decimated," and "victory" with my mineral pens. Now those words were scattered on the floor along with my pictures.

Hours and hours of time and effort, and Ehren had slashed them into pieces, leaving score marks on my bedroom walls from the knife.

Ehren reached for the last picture, the largest one pinned over my bed, the flag of the Vogt Faction. I'd worked on it for days, gluing the pages, drawing out the two-headed dragon just like I'd seen it on Freude's uniform, and colouring in the black, red, and yellow portions. I'd even done it on both sides, wanting to make it like a real flag.

"No, Ehren! That's mine," I shouted, diving at him.

He was too quick for me, and too big. He simply swept me aside with one hand as he ripped the flag down the middle.

"No, no, no," I kept repeating, flailing against his side. He just laughed.

Then I punched him in the balls, square and solid.

He doubled over, groaning and holding his belly. "You're gonna pay for that," he snarled.

I stood out of his reach, feet planted and fists clenched tight with fury and fear. Would Ehren pummel me now or bide his time? Ehren was apt to do either. He could be patient with his payback.

But he didn't do either. Instead, he glanced at Freude's schal, the ragged pile of red on my dresser. Ehren looked at me, looked back at the schal, waited until he knew I realised what would come next, and smiled. He snatched the schal in one hand and brandished Mum's paring knife in the other.

"Don't, Ehren." I held my voice even. My words came out crisp and dry like kindling.

My fists trembled, but not with fear. For the first time, I recognised a seed of ugliness growing inside me, a festering wound I hadn't noticed before. It fed on my anger, exhaustion, sadness, and fear—had been feeding on it, I realised, for months. Now, it germinated. My heart raced. My skin flushed. My thoughts scattered. I tasted its bitterness in my mouth like lye.

Ehren

"Or what?" Ehren taunted. "You'll cry?"

The ugly roots spread wide and deep and a different fear took me—the fear of what I might do. "Give it back now, Ehren."

He bared his teeth and snarled. "Come and get it."

He stabbed the blade into Freude's schal, and it bit and tore into the fabric. Threads split. Bits of lint drifted to the floor. When I saw it, I saw Freude. I saw that knife biting into him, tearing his flesh.

I charged Ehren, caught him by surprise and thrust my shoulder into his chest. We fell to the floor, the knife clattering from his hand. He tried to scramble away, but I leapt on his back. He flipped over, grabbed my shoulders, and tried to throw me off, but I didn't throw punches like he expected.

My hands went straight for his throat. They clamped down on his neck. He gripped my hands, nails digging into the backs and drawing blood. My torchlamp began to dim, a slow descent into darkness. In the yellow shadows, I saw the terror in his eyes, the surrender.

I wondered though, even as my hands gripped his

throat. Why is he letting me do this? Why give in? He's six years older, and me just a kid. Does he want to die?

I studied his face, a face so much like Mum's. Of the brothers, he was the handsomest. That handsome face changed colour to a deep shade of cinnamon.

"What in the burning sight of the Goddess do you think you're doing?" A deep voice bellowed.

Da ripped one of my hands away from Ehren's neck and gripped the wrist hard, despite the bandage on it. Then he jerked me off of Ehren's chest. Ehren rolled to his side coughing, and I hung from my da's grip like a trussed bird. Ehren rolled to a sitting position and prodded his throat.

"He tried to kill me," he choked.

"You destroyed my room!"

"He tried to kill me," he repeated.

"You hit me with a shovel!"

"He tried to kill me!" Ehren shouted as if it had just dawned on him what he'd been saying the whole time.

My da looked between us, from me to Ehren and back. He shook his head as if things weren't making sense to him, and I smelled the liquor on him.

And I'd thought he'd been finishing the chores...

"What's this about?" he asked.

"He tried-"

"Ehren got mad and-"

 "-hands around my neck-"

"-broke mum's mug."

Da dropped me. Surprised, my legs buckled, and I collapsed on the floor next to Ehren.

"You broke Mum's mug?" Da growled at Ehren. The waning light obscured his face. Deep shadows hung from his brows.

Ehren gawked at him, mouth swinging opened and closed like it had come loose. "No, he-"

"You. Broke. Her. Mug?" Da enunciated each word, a man jerking the knot tight on a hangman's noose.

"It was only because-"

"Freude would never have acted like that."

Da should have known better. He should have known what those words would do to Ehren.

Ehren's expression froze, and as I lay on the floor

watching him, his lips parted and spread into that grin that showed all his teeth. Before, I'd known what the grin meant. Now I knew what that grin felt like. Ehren had festering wounds too, and right now, I bet he tasted bitterness like lye.

"Freude is dead," Ehren answered.

Though he smiled and his teeth glinted in the yellow light, there was no smile to his eyes. The light fell through them, through two black holes into the ugly.

Da huffed at the reply, stumbled on his feet a little, too tired and too drunk to answer. Ehren and I looked at him and then glanced at each other. Something passed between us. Recognition? Understanding? Whatever it was, Ehren turned away.

The torchlamp waned, pitching the room into gloom. Ehren pushed himself to his feet. Freude's schal sat on the floor behind him. I stared at it as he helped Da out of the room and put him to bed. I could hear Da mumbling about Freude while Ehren tucked a blanket over him.

The next morning, I tripped over a box of Ehren's

toy soldiers sitting outside my bedroom door, cheap mimics shaped from wood and painted. Cheap or not, I'd coveted them my whole life. I gathered the box in my arms and padded softly down the hall to Ehren's room.

It was empty, the bed made.

Ehren never made his bed. Change the sheets, maybe throw a blanket over, but he never made it.

I crept to the living room, my grip tightening on the box. The corners dug into the creases of my elbows. Morning light split the room through the front window, turning the shadows darker and the things in the light blinding.

No Ehren.

Then the backdoor creaked and slammed, unlatched and swinging free in the wind. As I padded into the kitchen, it slammed again.

Ehren had cleaned up the crockery and tea while I slept. A new mug sat in place of the one he'd shattered. Same size. Same colour. Same clay. Freude had made that mug for him, but Ehren had even taken the trouble to chip the lip.

The door slammed again, closing then opening on a world bleached white by pure morning light. A distant, solitary figure hiked down the road and disappeared around the turn.

My throat tightened like a vice as I softly closed the door. Then I returned to the living room and set up each wooden figurine on the coffee table. I stared at them, memorised their faces and flaws like I'd never memorised Ehren's.

Hours later, well past noon, Da trudged past and muttered a question about Ehren's whereabouts. Instead of answering, I played with the figurines in silence. He looked at them. Looked at me. Clenched his jaw and trudged on.

Da didn't come home that night so I took care of chores all on my own. It took hours, but I did it. Me. Alone. That became the way of things from then on.

Meanwhile, Mum sewed up Freude's schal, cinched it up neat and tight like nothing had happened, nothing had changed, as if there never was a tear.

Chapter 17: Cracks in Paradise

∞

*It was hard not to turn away from that
man—not to bury my head in excuses
and hide from my weakness...*

∞

Morning breaks clear, the wind not yet churning dust and salt into the air. The temperature dropped enough in the night to leave my muscles stiff and my chest tight. Shivers make redressing my side wound shattering painful. It weeps yellowish fluid, and the flesh is swollen and sore. Not good.

After redressing my side wound, I ask Thirteen for a surveillance report. I can't hear in my sleep, but he can.

No one approached within twenty meters of our

camp during the night, but the neighbours fifty meters away complained about your snoring.

I roll my eyes but let him get away with the joke. If it weren't for Thirteen's constant sensory surveillance, I doubt I could sleep at night.

"Water?" I ask, picking up Freude's schal. I run my thumb over the almost imperceptible stitches that patched the tear Ehren made.

According to the maps I have available in my local archive, a freshwater well is located approximately 1.6 kilometres down the trail. Look for a long line of people trying their darnedest not to kill each other.

I wrap Freude's schal around my neck. It chafes, rough with sweat and grime, but it helps against the morning chill. I check my plague blade, then decide to stow it in the satchel instead of wear it. The nodes just hurt too much today. Then I shoulder the satchel and canteen.

"'Darnedest?' Really?"

I heard it yesterday. It sounded like fun to use, and I was right. It is fun!

I snort in amusement, heading to the trail and falling into a ground-eating trot.

"Darnedest... Darnedest..." I mutter to myself. I take a side trail that cuts closer to the river than the main refugee trail. Several other groups are already up and moving too even with the sun not quite risen. When I come up on them, they make way for the crazy guy. Sometimes talking to myself has its advantages.

I find the well. Like Thirteen said, there's a long line already. People shuffle along, bleary-eyed with exhaustion and hunger, but no one can live without freshwater. Once the Traege River reaches the Dustlands, the saltstone taints the water and turns it undrinkable.

I step into line. Several people line up after me. No jostling or scuffles. There'll be a few clinkers who decide to cut the line, but the rest of us just want to have our turn. It's as if we're in silent agreement—I'll wait if you wait.

Wait for water. Wait for a meal. Wait for loved ones to come home. Wait for peace. Wait to die. We're all just too damn used to waiting.

I guess those done waiting go and join one of the resistance groups. They can't wait to fight. They can't wait to die.

A young girl ahead of me, maybe four or five years old, holds her mom's hand. Her mom looks asleep on her feet, but the girl peers at me with slotted pupils. Wild tangles of hair fall into her pale eyes, her pupils narrowed to vertical slits against the morning sun. Her gaze holds mine, her expression searching without begging—she just can't hide the hunger.

I dig into my pocket, pull out a strauch chew, and hold it out to her. She takes it with her free hand and pops it into her mouth. No hesitation. Then she turns around and shuffles forward with her mother. She doesn't look at me again. But while I'm taking my turn at the well, there's a tug on my sleeve. The little girl holds out a feather to me. I take it.

The girl's mother fetches her, dragging her away with a glare at me. I can't blame her with there being so many slavers around, but I'm the least likely person to be a groomer. Groomers always look the least suspicious—a young girl who lost her parents, a crippled old man, a handsome lad with a sob story… Not someone like me who looks like a suffering drug addict or an ex-convict.

Come to think of it—technically, I'm both. I guess all of the above are good reasons to keep her daughter away from me.

I spin the feather between my finger and thumb. It's black with bluish iridescence like my hair. Judging by the length and symmetry, looks to be a tail feather from a frilled crow. The feathers are all over the place around here. Not hard to find. Not useful or valuable.

I stow it in the satchel anyway.

For not liking people, you seem to like kids, Thirteen observes.

"Kids seem more like pets than people at that age. I like animals." I pop a strauch chew into my mouth.

Canteen full again and another long day of walking ahead. There's an ache in my bones today and across my skin that worries me. Still, I adjust the strap of

Wilhelm's satchel and hitch up my trousers.

I won't die today. I won't. I-

Laughter?

The sound interrupts my personal pep talk. Laughter in this place with these people is like thunder on a sunny day. It doesn't belong.

I pursue the sound.

The main trail is the other way, Thirteen instructs, confused. He doesn't get it—doesn't understand why I have to find the laughter.

The sound leads me to the riverbank where two boys play. They grapple on the sand in front of the water. Their oversized pack sits nearby with nothing but their boots and socks guarding it.

The older boy wears layers of clothes despite the heat—a half-cloak with a high collar and baggy sleeves, trousers, a schal that comes up over his chin and mouth, and a flat cap to cover his hair. The oddest part of his getup is the gloves. He wears fitted leather gloves on both hands like a high-class rider or a mounted cavalryman might. They clasp at his wrists and extend to the middle of his forearms.

The younger boy, much younger by the looks of it, wears half as much, just a filthy undershirt tucked into trousers cinched to his skinny waist with a belt. Seems he was wearing a button-up shirt over the undershirt, but it lays in the sand off to the side now.

I decide to cut the kids some slack and settle down near enough to their pack and shoes that thieves will think twice. I set down Wilhelm's satchel, placing my noisy canteen on top of it as a sort of alarm, and pull off my boots and socks.

What are you doing? Thirteen asks, perplexed.

I smirk. "You said I stink, didn't you? Now's my chance to fix that."

Here? Now? Will it even make a difference?

"It won't make your stink meter go higher so no harm done."

Fine. Wash your socks too then.

I shake my head in amusement. "You're lucky we share the same nose and mouth, Thirteen. If you had your own, you can just guess where these socks would go."

If it meant I had my own mouth and nose, I'd gladly accept.

Thirteen says it like a jest, but I sense some bitterness in the words. I hated having voices in my head—what would it be like to be a voice without a body?

A splash. The younger boy succeeded in tripping the older one into the water. The kid taunts him. The older one dives for the younger, trying to drag him into the water, too.

"Brothers," I say.

What about brothers? Thirteen asks.

"Those two, they're brothers."

How can you tell? They don't look alike.

He's right. The kid's skin is medium brown while the young man's is pale. The kid's eyes are icy blue while the young man's are a piercing black. Black hair versus brown. A round face with a small sloping nose as compared to a pointed chin and a narrow pointed nose.

The only similar features between them are their eye shapes—large round eyes with pronounced epicanthal folds, like Wilhelm's eyes. Even then, the kid's eyes are monolid while the young man's has a partial crease.

"I just can," I reply to Thirteen. It's the only reply I can give. Despite the differences, I can tell it's there—the sibling bond. The love and the hate.

The younger brother seems to have gotten the better of the older. The older brother removes his cloak and tosses it aside, revealing an overlarge button-up shirt and suspenders. The scuffle goes up a notch. The older brother's shirt comes untucked from his trousers and one of his suspenders falls from his shoulder. Then his little brother swipes his flat cap, revealing a top bun that's become something of a snarled mane.

It's the top bun that rings a bell. Thirteen and I realise it at the same time—the two kids who escaped the train before the explosion.

"Thirteen-" I start.

It's them, the kids from the train. They escaped!

To my surprise, Thirteen sounds sincerely happy to

see them. With the way he acted when we first saw them by the train, I assumed he'd be indifferent at best. I guess I really am always his first priority.

Leviatan, the anzug users.

"Agreed. Perform a scan." I stand and act like I'm stretching, making a lazy circle to give Thirteen a panoramic view of our surroundings.

Done. No signs of surveillance, but that's not to say there isn't any.

"Those anzug users weren't following them just to watch. If they aren't here now, it's because the kids lost them, or they weren't after the kids in the first place."

As I recall, allowing your targets to believe they lost you so they let down their guard is standard practice. You've used it more than once.

"Those anzug users aren't me."

No, but they could be sent by the man who trained you.

I cringe at the well-aimed reminder. With Bann after me, I shouldn't take anything for-granted. But still, the anzug users weren't after me to begin with. It looked like they were after these two kids, and the more I watch them, the more I wonder why. What kind of mess are they in that they have to hop trains and dodge anzug users?

I set to washing my socks, but my attention keeps wandering to those two brothers. I hardly notice the saltwater saturating the wraps on my arms and stinging the nodes.

The older brother catches the younger and drags him into the water, but the younger brother squirms and bucks, soaking them both and kicking up dust from the shore. I think I'd be swearing by now, but the young man just laughs. When his little brother escapes his grasp entirely, leaving him alone in the water, he's still smiling.

"Du klines shvine," he shouts in exasperation. "Tzee kommen har."

His voice is higher than I expected. The language he uses seems familiar, but the words slip away before I grasp them.

Narrisch, Thirteen offers. *A dialect of Manual*

common to the steppes region of the Reichland.

Steppes region? Bergverk. No wonder it sounds familiar.

The little brother stands several meters away in his mud-caked clothes. His chest heaves, accentuating his protruding ribs. Muddy, clothes in tatters, hair wild—he reminds me of a cunning little beastie up to no good. His blue eyes gleam with mischief.

"Mikael, tzee kommen har bitte," the older brother beckons.

The beast-child shakes his head, planting his feet and placing his hands on hips.

"Tzee kommen heehar zerook," his older brother yells, patience gone. The little brother sticks his tongue out at him and disappears into the trees. The older brother throws his hands in exasperation.

His words trickle through my mind. I can't grasp their meaning, but I'm sure Thirteen is already working on a translation.

My canteen suddenly clangs shifting on the satchel. The young man turns abruptly toward me, startled.

When our eyes meet, his smile fades. He doesn't say anything—I don't either—but I see his guard go up. His eyes remind me of a bird's, so dark a brown they look black, and the look in them is keen and careful. He fetches his brother's shirt and his own cloak and hat, tugging his hat back onto his head and pulling it low over his eyes. Then he scrubs his brother's shirt with sand. It's a poor substitute for soap, but better than nothing.

I nod toward the young man and subvocalize to Thirteen. 'What do you think of him, Thirteen?'

My data indicates an 86% probability he is a refugee.

'And the other fourteen percent?'

Spy or assassin. If he takes the initiative and engages you in conversation, that probability increases to 26%.

The young man stands, laundry in hand. He says something to me, but I can't hear him over the river.

Warning! He initiated conversation.

"What?" I call back, ignoring Thirteen.

"Is it good in rinsing now?" he shouts back. His Northern accent lengthens the "oo" and softens the n's and d's. "It will not"—he searches for a word—"be annoying you?"

I look at him blankly.

Be careful, Thirteen warns. *I'm sure he's planning to strangle you with that filthy shirt.*

I can't tell if Thirteen is being serious or sarcastic, but his comment at least clarifies the situation. The shirt. I'm downstream. He doesn't want to rinse the sand out until I'm done.

"Go ahead. I'm finished," I blurt, squeezing out my socks.

The young man nods. He sits on his haunches a couple meters away and drags his brother's shirt through the water. I study him. As I watch, he reaches too far into the water and loses his balance, nearly goes in headlong. He catches himself, but yelps, snatching at something in the water. His brother's shirt floats out of reach, carried downstream by the current. I reach out and snag it as it passes me.

I laugh mockingly. Yes, Thirteen, definitely an assassin.

The young man runs up to me, panting. "Danke," he says.

Language analysis complete, Thirteen announces.

Suddenly, I know that word—know that it's 'thank you.' It twists in my mind like a key unlocking the language. And Bergverk comes with it.

Screaming. Blood. Burning bodies. The memories intrude suddenly. I stumble and sit in the sand.

The young man studies me. "Mein Herr, are you, uh, fine?" he asks.

Slowly I sit back, a bit dizzy and my side aching. I blink until I can see clearly again.

My canteen clatters. The sound of someone getting into the satchel! I lash out behind me, palm open. My hand strikes flesh forcefully, and the little brother is knocked backward, landing on his rear in the dirt, stunned.

Of all the things he could grab from Wilhelm's satchel, he clutches my plague blade. I try to take it from him, but he makes a run for it. I catch his wrist—the one holding my plague blade—and lift him into the air. The boy bares his teeth at me, like a good beast child should.

"Let go of my brother!" The young man yells in Narrisch. He lunges for a tree branch and brandishes it at me, but Thirteen starts yelling at the same time.

Assassin! Assassin! Thirteen hollers. *Dodge left! Dodge left!*

I pull the little brother into a hug—keep tight hold of the wrist with the blade—and dodge left, expecting the tree branch to brush past me. Instead, I catch the tree branch full in the face.

Dodge right, you idiot.

'You said left!'

Right!

I duck right this time. Again, a branch prickly with strauch needles smacks me in the head.

Thirteen cackles gleefully. *You were right—I said left. Left was right!*

"Thirteen," I growl between my clenched teeth.

He continues to cackle.

At this point, I turn my back to the older brother and just accept the tree branch thrashing. Meanwhile, the kid claws at my hand trying to get free of me. Finally, the older brother slows and lowers the branch, panting.

"Finished?" I ask, turning around.

"Let go of my brother," he says again, this time in heavily accented Common.

"He tried to steal my stuff," I reply.

He answers slowly, assembling the words between gulps of air. "But he...did not...steal."

"Attempted theft is still a crime," I reply.

"Not...here," he retorts.

He has a point, Thirteen says. *Dustlander law indicates that a crime must be accomplished to be a crime.*

"You stay out of this," I snarl. The young man's brow scrunches in concern, but he doesn't say anything. Can he tell the comment wasn't directed at him? I look the older brother in the eye and speak in Narrisch. "If I put this kid down, he won't steal from me again?"

The young man folds his arms across his chest and raises an eyebrow, using scepticism to hide his surprise that I know Narrisch. He answers in Narrisch. "If he does, what will you do? Carry him all the way to Rettung?"

Thirteen snickers. *Good point.*

I smile coldly. "Maybe I'll just cut off his hands…"

The kid hanging in my grasp curses and kicks at me. I catch his ankle with my free hand and hang him upside-down. He drops my plague blade in surprise. He hollers, clawing at me blindly. He snags Freude's schal and pulls it off, dropping it into the dirt. Then his dirty undershirt comes untucked and slides up over his face, exposing his torso.

Black stains envelop his back. Hollowbern stains. Like trails of smoke, they cover large swathes of his chest and back in curling tendrils of black and grey.

I think of Perri and the black vein-like stains that patterned her face. The kid is lucky his stains only mark his chest and back. As long as he keeps them covered, no one will be able to tell he's not a Lowly.

I glance at the kid's older brother and realise that with the way he's covered, he's probably a hollowbern too.

Two hollowbern boys escaping the Reichland... Is that why they've had to hop trains and dodge anzug users? I helped the Vogt and their Neo-Arkist allies take over Bergverk. It's my fault these brothers are on the run.

My head aches, memories threatening to spill into the present.

I put the kid down and he runs to his older brother. I put my hand to my head, pressing my temples to ease a piercing headache. Vertigo takes hold and I stumble to one knee. Thirteen calls, but his voice seems very far away.

The pain finally recedes. Then I realise the older brother is kneeling beside me. He's pinching the inner ridge of my ear.

"Better?" he asks, studying my face.

I nod.

Huh, Thirteen sounds impressed. *He used your daith*

pressure point to subdue your migraine. He makes a throat-clearing sound. *Not that that is all that impressive. I could do that if I had hands.*

"Sorry," the older brother says, looking embarrassed. "My brother is hungry. It made him stupid for a moment."

He stands. I expect him to take his brother and leave after that, but he picks up Freude's red schal instead. He brushes the sand from it and plucks off a few twigs. Then he hangs it around my neck, ties it in a neat knot at the front like a scarf. The moment feels familiar...

"Rot fuur glook," he murmurs and steps back. Red for luck.

Freude.

After all I've been through, my heart can still ache.

The young man nods and walks to his little brother. He smacks his brother on the back of the head for good measure. They immediately start to bicker.

What does it mean, to not turn away?

"Wait," I say.

The older brother stops and turns, dark eyes

questioning and somewhat wary.

What? Did you spot korrectives or something? I didn't see anything...

"Food," I tell the brother.

Food? We have food.

The brother stares at me quizzically.

"For you," I say.

His eyes widen in surprise.

Leviatan, this is a bad idea. Unless it is for some survival advantage, it is better we don't engage with others, particularly these two. It greatly increases to probability of a report reaching the Vogt.

Thirteen is right. This is a bad idea. But just this once, I want to see what it's like. Wilhelm's daughter wrote that it matters. I want to know if she's right. I want to know if it makes a difference—not turning away.

"If it comes down to it, I can always leave," I reply to Thirteen quietly. Of course I can leave. Leaving is easy. It's all I've ever known.

Then I take a deep breath and shore up my resolve.

"I'll help you find food," I say in Narrisch.

After a moment's hesitation, the older brother's shoulders finally relax. The wind blows, whipping his cloak and schal. I glimpse his lips. They're chapped, dried blood in the creases, but he's smiling.

For the first time, I realise some things are beautiful even when they're broken. No, not broken. Breaking. Breaking but persisting anyway.

That's how brothers should be.

Chapter 18: The Hunter and the Fool

∞

...but all I could do for him was watch.
All I had to offer was to not turn away.

∞

I lead the two brothers to a clutch of mangroves growing into the river like a peninsula. The river narrows on the far side, flowing swiftly between the mangroves and a saltstone ledge on the opposite bank. The water is deep here. That and the tangles of mangrove roots would make falling in a mighty dangerous thing.

I leave my boots and Freude's schal with Wilhelm's satchel on the bank. The low, tangled branches of the mangroves won't allow for any extra baggage. The two brothers stand nearby, watching me.

I stand and wave a hand at the satchel and boots. "Watch it for me?"

The older brother looks at it, then at me, and nods. His posture relaxes. He's relieved I've left something with them, something for me to come back for.

I step into the mangroves and set my feet on a thick, slick root. I wiggle my toes. The day has already turned hot, but the spray spilling across the mangroves feels icy.

Leviatan, what are you doing? Thirteen asks.

"Hunting," I answer.

For...

"Food."

Thirteen issues an overlong sigh, letting me know he understands I'm not going to elaborate and that annoys him.

The older brother steps up beside me. He steps on the roots in his bare feet and reaches above his head to grip the branches. His pack, cloak, and boots wait on the ground beside my own.

I look down at him and speak in Common. "What are you doing?"

"Food," he says, cocking his head to the side.

"No, you wait here," I respond.

He jerks his chin toward the mangroves, a gesture for me to continue and his intention to continue with me. He must not have understood.

I point at him. "You." I open my hand, the palm toward him. "Wait." I point at my satchel. "Here."

He turns to his brother. "Mikael," he says. He points at his brother. "You." Throws his palm out. "Wait." And points at the satchel. "Here." He uses my same intonations despite a heavy Reichlander accent. I can't decide if he's making fun of me or not.

The younger brother glares at us and sits hard on the ground beside our stuff. The older brother turns back at me.

"Give a man to fish…," he says in Narrisch and shrugs.

I know that one! 'Give a man a fish and feed him for a day. Teach a man to fish and feed him for life.' I like that one. It has an actual rational basis, unlike 'a clear conscience is a soft pillow.' That just makes no sense.

I sigh and roll my eyes. I don't feel up to arguing, with Thirteen or with the older brother. Hopefully the promise of food is enough to convince the younger brother not to steal my stuff. This won't take long anyway.

Upstream of the mangroves, the water moves slowly, but the mangrove roots make swimming treacherous. It looks serene, but the water and mangrove roots can pin and drown a person. On the other side of the mangrove, the river ripples and eddies as it flows out of the roots. On this side, the currents are the threat, likely to carry a person down and pin him at the bottom of the river.

"Don't get close to the water," I call over my shoulder in Narrisch. "If you slip, grab hold of anything to not go in. I won't save you if you do. Got it?"

I don't hear an answer.

"Got it?" I call louder.

"Yes," the young man replies.

Would you really not save him? Thirteen asks curiously.

"Let's hope I never have to answer that."

Which means you would save him, you just don't want to argue. He sounds sulky when he says it.

The thing is, I can't tell if he's put out because I'm willing to risk us to save someone or because I don't want to argue. Strange AI…

The Dustlands don't have a particularly diverse ecology, but certain places become menageries of life, particularly the oases in the desert and the mangroves on the river. Microraptors, frilled crows, sperlings, and other flying creatures often nest in the branches, which attracts predators like urvogels, compsos, and serpents, as well as scavengers, like long-toothed cynodonts, prowlers, and spined rats.

Then there are the water creatures. The water surrounding the mangroves has a higher salt concentration since the mangroves take the water and leave the salt. The beasties who prefer these salty depths have cousins that roam the oceans.

The Hunter and the Fool

There are dangers, but I spent more than a little time around these mangroves as a kid. I've learned since then that people are far scarier.

"Move slowly," I instruct in Narrisch over my shoulder. "Watch where you put your feet and hands. The critters will run as long as you give them time to."

I move through the mangroves, the older brother close behind. The first nest isn't far from shore. I search for the microraptor male since it guards the nest while the female hunts. I don't see it in the canopy.

Actually, I don't see any beasties in the canopy. A few frilled crows perch in the strauch trees on shore, their heads cocked to watch me, and a few more circle above the mangroves. I peer at them through the branches. They look back, watching silently.

The silence and that look, they put me on edge.

Leviatan, the animals are acting strangely.

"Agreed," I answer back.

I creep even more slowly through the mangroves, slipping my hand into the unguarded nest. My fingers find only a smooth mud bowl. It's empty. Not even an egg shell or feather left.

The young man sees what I'm after and moves off in the other direction to search nests. After a few minutes, I hear him call excitedly. He waves a blue-speckled egg in the air and smiles brightly. He tucks the egg into a sling he's made with his schal and searches more enthusiastically. Reminds me of a kid doing an egg hunt at the Spring Mondlikt Festival.

I move to the next nest, but it's also empty. So are the next and next. How come he's found one but I haven't?

Somehow, this also reminds me of Mondlikt Festival. I was never any good at the egg hunts. I preferred the petting zoo instead.

I climb, getting anxious. I grip the overhead branches and wedge my feet into forking trunks, to search for nests. The curve of an egg, blue and speckled brown, peeks from a nest a few meters away.

Finally!

I scramble for it, branches scratching my face and roots tearing at my toes. I squirm between the trees like a child, excited to finally have some success.

My foot slips, but I catch myself on a branch, a sturdy one as thick as my arm. It gives slightly, stretching, helping me right myself. I climb down and look for an easier way to reach the nest.

The boy on the bank is yelling.

"What's he saying?" I ask absently, massaging my arm where I hit the branch.

I need a visual. The water is interfering with the sound.

I peer through the tangled mangrove trunks, surprised to see the boy not only shouting but waving his arms and running back and forth on the bank. He waves at his older brother, but it seems his brother hasn't noticed yet.

"Thirteen, what's he saying?" I ask.

Leviatan... He is yelling for his sibling to run.

"Run? Why?" I murmur, more to myself than to Thirteen. Then, from the corner of my eye, the branch that saved me slides back into the canopy, scales glistening on it in contrast with the smooth trunks of the mangroves.

It wasn't a branch at all.

I grab for the crappy little pocketknife I keep clipped to my trousers.

Behind, Thirteen warns.

I flip out the knife and spin. The blade strikes a crocodilian snout that snaps shut beside my head. I retreat through the trees, a slow process while trying to not fall in and watch the canopy. The canopy shakes as the beast follows after me.

A giant serpent? No, I glimpse short legs propelling the serpentine body through the canopy. It's a giant skink. The size of it stuns me. Judging by the tail I accidently grabbed and the size of its head, the creature might be six or seven meters long.

I slow to navigate a tricky section near the water, and the creature takes the chance to strike again. Mandibles twitch on either side of its jaw. I slash wildly, clipping the beast's snout and opening a shallow gash. It jerks away, hissing. I try to backpedal away, knife up in case it strikes again, but my foot slips. My leg drops between roots, and my crotch hits hard. The pain steals my breath.

I want to laugh at the absurdity of it. After all I've been through this is how I go, eaten by a giant lizard after wracking myself. I'd get points for creativity.

Leviatan, Thirteen warns, sounding frantic. *What are you doing? Move!*

But my leg is caught between the roots. I can't get it free. Lights Above, this might be it. I bring my pocketknife up in a guard position.

The beast lunges, mouth wide-

Something glances off its eye. The object clangs and glitters as it falls into the roots. A dagger?

The skink jerks away, snarling, a shallow gash opening on its eyelid. I twist around.

The older brother stands a several meters away. One of his gloved hands grips the trunk of a mangrove, and the other hand is extended in mid-air. It was a hell of a throw, his thin arm deceptively strong. Too bad it missed.

The beast spots the brother, too.

I shout, trying to draw its attention back, but it ignores me. Instead, it cocks its head, studying the new arrival. Then it looks back at me. Almost like... Like it's weighing its options.

My skin crawls. "Thirteen, what are we actually dealing with here?"

This creature does not match any description of native species.

"Which means?"

This is most likely a golem.

"Like the elephant at Bergverk?"

No, that one was abnormal. Most golems are like this—highly intelligent and aggressive.

The creature watches my mouth when I talk. Highly intelligent... I shudder. I don't dare make a move. "What is it doing here?"

Not much is known about golems. They are a form of existence rather than a specific species. They appear randomly as an individual specimen, breed with a compatible native species, producing non-golem hybrid offspring, and die.

The Hunter and the Fool

It appears randomly and in as a random species. No wonder Thirteen said the golem at the banquet was abnormal.

According to my records, this specimen is a mere Level Two golem. There are records of much larger specimens. There is a reason golem-hunting is a profession. Over one-hundred and thirty hunters die-

The golem sets its eyes on the older brother and seems to come to a decision.

"Save the trivia for later," I interrupt.

The idiot brother hasn't even recovered from throwing the dagger yet. He stands there with his arm in the air like a shattering fool.

"Run!" I shout.

White scales whip past me as the beast goes after him. Its many legs heave its massive body through the canopy. The young man tries to scramble away. He slips and the skink dives at him, but he clambers to his feet and uses a branch to swing and launch himself forward. The skink plows into the roots where he was. It thrashes, short legs struggling to pull it back into the canopy.

The desperate swing nearly launches the young man into the water. He flails at the edge of the mangroves on the downstream side.

No. No. No... The word repeats in my mind, my only thought as I climb to my feet and sprint for him.

The beast lunges for him so the young man lets himself fall. His body enters the water as the skink's jaws snap shut on empty air.

I race for the water, ready to dive in after him. I jump.

The golem, Thirteen says. It's all he has time to say.

I twist in the air as the beast strikes. Its head darts beneath me, but the thick neck catches me across the chest, batting me out of the air. I crash onto the mangrove roots, feet dangling in the river.

The skink coils around me like a giant serpent. I strike at its scales with my pocketknife, but the blade glances off uselessly. Of course it would. The scales are armour, like my koganzug.

"Thirteeeee…" The skink squeezes the air out of me.

I can't talk. I could subvocalize, but it's hard to thing straight with so much pain.

I reach for the Ugly in the pit of my stomach, that anger that has saved me many times before, but it isn't there. That inhuman part of me isn't there; yet, I'm reaching for it, hoping it can save me.

Weak spots! Thirteen shouts in my mind. *Find a weak spot!*

Where would its armour be weak? Where would it have the fewest scales? I should know this. How much time did I spend as a kid messing around with natters and the like?

Finally, I remember. Like my koganzug armour, it's where it needs the most flexibility!

The crocodilian face approaches my head, mandibles chittering and mouth stretching wide.

The mouth!

I drive my knife upward into its throat, right at the point where the jaw meets the neck. I lock my other arm around the crocodilian head at the same time. The thrust parts the small, weak scales, allows the knife to go right up through the airway and pass through the roof of the mouth into the head.

The beast tries to crush me. My ribs ache with the strain, ready to shatter. The wound in my side bursts open, blood hot on my skin. Long weeks of bandages, medicine, and coaxing the wound to heal, completely wasted.

The beast writhes, but I grip its head tighter and thrust the blade in a second time, then a third. The beast finally collapses. I collapse with it, gasping for air, its snout resting only a few centimetres from my head.

Grey splotches spread across the shimmering scales like a blight and darken to lustreless black. Then the skin crumbles like the elephant at Bergverk, and I stare in fascinated horror as the carcass disintegrates from around my body, turning into piles of Dust.

This is the Dustlands—my homeland of monsters and nightmares, of dust and Dust.

Welcome home, Leiden.

The wind blows, snatching up the piles of Dust and scattering them into the river—a fortune gone in an instant. But I don't have time to care because that shattering idiot is still at the bottom of the river.

I climb back to my feet, take a deep breath, and dive into the water.

Chapter 19: In Too Deep

∞

The Elders taught me that darkness is borne of inaction. I could not abandon him to darkness.

∞

With Thirteen's guidance, I navigate the currents to shore, towing the older brother with me. His body is heavy, far heavier than I expected.

When we reach the shallows, he spews and the water carries the vomit away. It's a good thing—a belly full of saltwater from the Traege could poison him.

No one else comes to our aid. It'd be hard to hear us over the river, and even if anyone did, they all have enough troubles of their own. I'm the only fool who'd rather take on someone else's troubles than deal with my own.

We collapse on the shore, both of us gulping down air. It's just me and him.

The boy is coming, Thirteen informs me.

Aw, the kid. He's going to be pissed.

And he is—screams obscenities at me, blaming me for putting his brother at risk—but I'm too tired to care. All of me hurts, and blood continues to trickle from my side wound. If he wants to yell, then yell. Not like I can hear him much over the thundering in my ears anyway.

Thirteen murmurs something about the kid.

Can't hear him. Can't hear much of anything.

"Hey!"

There's a roaring in my ears—like the constant crash of ocean waves—that drowns out everything else.

"Hey!"

A hand on my shoulder shakes me. A voice calls from far away, frantic, but I'm too tired to answer.

A bitter scent sears my nose, chases away the exhaustion and darkness. I cough, my eyes watering.

The older brother sits beside me holding a small vial to my nose.

"Okay?" he asks, eyes tight with worry.

I try to sit up, but he forces me back down.

"You're hurt." He speaks in Narrisch, too worried to stumble over Common. He tries to pull up my bloody shirt to look at the wound. But if he does, he'll see the nodes, too.

I brush off his hands. "No."

"Yes, I can help," he says. "I have medical training."

"No, it's fine." I sit up, but a sudden rushing in my head and searing pain in my side force me to gasp.

You should let him look. He says he has training, and even if he doesn't, we won't be any worse off than we are now.

The young man pulls at my shirt again. This time, I let him look.

I shake my head. "Why bother?"

The question is for Thirteen, but it's for the older brother too. I don't understand why the older brother is being so insistent. We're surrounded by people who need help. Their graves mark the trail, saltstone shards piled up like cairns.

"You're worth saving," the older brother answers.

I'm worth it? Because I saved him? Is my life of value only because he values his own? It makes sense, but the logic bothers me.

A spell of light-headedness hits me, and I close my eyes. Hot, midday sun falls over my face, but goose bumps prickle my skin.

It appears from your vitals that we are going into shock, Thirteen says, sounding concerned.

"Hm," I answer.

You should stay awake, he adds.

"Hm," I answer again.

Leviatan...

"Just let him die," the younger brother says from somewhere far away.

I can't hear the reply.

"Just look at him! As soon as he finds out about us, he'll turn us in."

Again, a murmured reply.

"You're a fool. No wonder Pops left us behind."

His words are harsh, but I understand them. It's not himself he's worried about—harsh words like that come out when we're scared for the other person. It's the weapon we use when trust isn't enough.

Something cool touches my forehead. I open my eyes. The older brother leans over me, his hand pressed to my forehead. His hair, long and loose now after our brushes with death, tickles my neck. He grimaces in frustration before sitting back and using his schal to tie his hair back. Then he gently presses two fingers to my wrist, checking my pulse. He closes his eyes to concentrate.

I stare at his face. The sun behind him creates a halo effect, but I still see the bruises shadowing his eyes and the dirt darkening the creases of stress on his face.

He's not as young as I first thought. Thin bones, thin features, sharp chin and cheeks and nose. Built like a bird. Plus he has big black eyes with thick, long lashes. That's why I thought he was young.

But he's not young; he's a big brother. He knows

what it means to be a big brother, and he's known it for a long time.

"Why do you want to help me?" I ask in Narrisch.

"Wait," he says. He stands and I close my eyes as the sun strikes my face. It's only a minute or two before he comes back, draping a wet cloth across my forehead. Then he answers. "You didn't have to help us, but you did. Even after we wronged you, you tried."

"You don't owe-"

"This isn't about owing you. It's like..." He pauses, brow creased as he tries to work out his thoughts. "It's like the world is ugly enough as it is. The least I can do is something I'm able to—to add a little good where I can. Because I can." He shrugs helplessly. "Because I can, I want to try."

I try because I can, Thirteen says thoughtfully. Why he said it aloud, I'm not sure. Another odd habit or is he saying it for my benefit?

"I try because I can," I repeat.

The young man smiles sheepishly and nods. Then the younger brother arrives carrying their overlarge pack, Wilhelm's satchel, and Freude's schal around his neck. The older brother lifts off the pack and digs through it. He lays out a blanket and retrieves a surprisingly complete medical kit. He takes a small bottle from the kit, opens it, and hands it to me.

"Medicinal wine, an anaesthetic. Drink-"

I take it and down the bottle.

"-half," he finishes, cringing apologetically. "Don't blame me for the hangover."

The alcohol goes down like a wire brush, easily 130 proof, and the effects hit me like a rockslide within minutes. My head feels stuffed with wool, and it's hard to stay upright. He helps me to the clean blanket on the ground, his makeshift operating table.

"Shirt," he says.

I should worry about him seeing my implants, but I'm too far gone. I obey, put my arms up like a child, and he loosens the laces and pulls my shirt over my head. Then he helps me lay down. As he cleans my wound, he notices the nodes. His hand freezes. I wait for the questions.

"I'll clean those too," he says simply. That's all. He continues cleansing my wound.

Huh, Thirteen responds, amused. *I like him.*

My relief is a tipping point. I relax into the blanket and allow the wine to immerse my senses. There's a ringing in my ears, and my head aches. Better to let it all fade away.

"What should I call you?" the brother asks.

Call me? What should he call me...

"Freude," I say, slurring.

Freude? Why Freude? Thirteen asks. But I'm already too far gone to answer.

Last I remember is telling the young man that the teapot was broken and my schal was torn and my brother was gone. All gone.

That older brother, he held my hand and told me it would be okay. He said everything would be okay.

Liar.

I guess that never changes. All brothers are liars.

Chapter 20: Keim

Seven years and ten months ago.

After Ehren left, the house got quiet, and not the good kind. Da spent most of his time in town. Mum, mostly in bed. Keim worked and helped with chores, but then he holed up in his room with his gadgets the rest of the time.

Freude's death stole our hearts while Ehren's absence robbed us of our voices.

I did my best to fill the silence—to make the house feel not quite so empty—to try to make things a little more like they should have been.

I rested on my stomach on the floor beneath the coffee table, chin propped on my hands and wind howling in the shutters. Lying on the floor, I could smell the dust trapped between the floorboards and feel the grit on my skin. The staccato taps of Keim's pencil played counterpoint to the tinks of sand and sticks pelting the windows.

Keim studied at the dinner table. Normally, he'd have been in his room, except his room was on the windward side of the house, and Mum didn't like him in there during storms like this one.

Mum and Da worked somewhere out there in that sand, trying to get the beasties into the barn. On a bad day, it would've been me and Keim.

I contemplated the wooden figurines before me, my mind absorbed in a fantasy. Ehren's toy soldiers faced down Keim's stuffed toy elephant. He let me borrow it sometimes. It towered over the soldier figurines, and they desperately mowed it down before it could clobber them. Even then, the elephant's collapse took out the first rank of soldiers, and they scattered on the floor.

I gazed at the toys, my thoughts wandering. Was this how Freude died? He died in a war, and Mum said gods would use elephants to fight wars, and only a god could kill Freude.

That means if elephants are real, then Freude really died—my childish mind reasoned—but if elephants aren't real, there's no way the gods could kill him. Then Freude must be alive!

My fingers traced the nappy fabric of the stuffed toy. A blast of wind rattled the windows, shook dust down on us from the rafters.

"Hey, Keim!" I shouted from beneath the coffee table.

"What?" Keim replied, refusing to glance away from his books. A knot of muscle formed at his jaw.

"Are elephants real?" I asked.

Keim would know. He knew all sorts of interesting facts, like how stuff worked, how to build stuff, how to make stuff work better… He'd know if elephants were real.

He shook his head in annoyance, muttering to himself.

I clamoured over the couch and stood directly in

front of his desk, holding his stuffed elephant out to him, determined. "Keim! There's no way elephants are real, right?"

"Lights Above, get that stupid toy out of my face!" Keim shouted, slapping the back of my head. "Why don't you just grow up already!"

I sat on the floor in shock, the back of my head tingling from the strike of Keim's open palm. "But, Keim..." I whimpered.

That night, Keim came into my room. When I heard him I pretended to sleep, afraid he was still angry, but he didn't pour water on me or stick a herp down my back like I expected. He just stood at the end of my bed and cried.

I stayed silent.

After a few minutes, Keim set something beside my bed and left, closing the door behind him so that all the light from the hallway disappeared.

I slid out of bed and snatched my torchlamp from off my dresser. With a few quick twists, I wound it up. When I clicked it on, it illuminated the soft fabric of

Keim's stuffed elephant. He'd left a note beneath the toy saying that elephants were real.

I snatched it and tumbled back into bed, curling around my new treasure beneath the sheets.

I held it against my chest, trying to push away the ugly feelings inside me because the gift didn't mean Keim was sorry for smacking me. The gift meant Keim was sorry he was leaving. Not tomorrow or the next day, but soon.

First, Freude. Then, Ehren. Now, Keim.

Because elephants are real.

I hugged the toy harder, missing my brothers more than I missed anything in the whole wide world.

Chapter 21: Immaculate

∞

*There is action in seeing. There is light in
not turning away. There is power in
innocence when it becomes rage.*

∞

I wake with a start and a headache. The memory of
Keim is there at the forefront of my mind, but I push it
to the back of my thoughts. The present is too
disconcerting, too threatening, to contemplate it. My
brothers abandoned me, left me alone with our broken
parents. That's clear enough. No need to dwell on it.

It's the hour before the scamp moon rises, the
beginning and darkest part of the night. Supposedly, it's
the time when the scamp moon performs his mischief.

Immaculate

The sister moon sits on the horizon in her last quarter, and the fire near me has burned to embers. How long was I unconscious?

A canteen and cup wait for me beside the blanket along with my shirt, the holes stitched and the ragged edges trimmed. I fill and drain the cup several times, but my mouth still feels like I've had a rag stuffed in it. The night air feels chill on my feverish skin. I toss logs onto the embers to get the fire burning again.

The boy sleeps on the other side of the fire. He hugs the overlarge pack like a pillow, a ragged quilt thrown over him. His older brother is nowhere in sight.

My wound aches when I sit up, feeling like I've been skinned alive, but when I peep beneath the gauze wrapping, and the wound looks good. The stiches are tidy where it could be stitched, and it's packed well where the flesh will have to grow back in. Seems the young man was telling the truth about being trained.

I'll know for sure in the next few days—will my fever break and the healing begin or will the wound ooze and swell?

I pull on my shirt but don't bother with the ties or my suspenders and pull on my boots.

"Thirteen?" I ask. "Anything to report?"

It has been four hours since the conclusion of your procedure. The siblings argued after your surgery. The boy did not agree with his sibling's actions. The older individual left after the boy fell asleep.

What was so urgent he left his little brother behind? So many things could go wrong around here when someone's left alone. Maybe he didn't mean to go far? What if something happened to him?

I have the suspicion that the older brother-

"Which direction did the older brother go?"

Into the strauch trees near the ravine. The older youth seems-

"How long ago?"

Approximately half-an-hour. As I was saying-

"Later, Thirteen. This is a bad time to be wandering. That kid is going to get himself mugged."

But I think this is import-

A shift in the shadows outside the reach of the

firelight catches my attention. It's in the same direction Thirteen said the older brother went.

"Later," I order.

I squint, barely making out the shape of a person as it enters the strauch trees.

"Thirteen, did you see that?"

If you did, I did.

"Was it the older brother?"

The lighting is too dim to confirm upon review but based on approximate stature, it seems unlikely.

"Not many people wander this time of night. I better check it out."

Suit yourself. Not like you listen to me anyway.

I roll my eyes.

I'm a little unsteady after hauling myself up, still drunk from the wine, but I get my feet under me and head in the direction the figure went. The scamp moon rises, illuminating the landscape in a pink glow and providing enough light to navigate by. The scamp moon rises and sets at the same time year-round so that puts the time around eight at night.

People in the Dustlands don't much bother with timekeepers. Between the sun, the phases of the sister moon, and the passage of the scamp moon, we know what time it is near enough to count.

When I was stuck in hospital after my surgery, I heard a story about the moons. Supposedly, they were siblings. The scamp moon was the sister moon's little brother, and he liked to cause all sorts of trouble and was never on time for his rises or sets.

One night, he tugged a thread that unravelled the sky. Stars fell and hit the World. The World was furious and wanted to cast out the little red moon, but his older sister stood up for him. As soon as the World met her, it fell in love with the sister moon. The World asked to marry her, and, to save her brother, she agreed. After his sister married the World, the scamp moon could see her only once a night and that was only for half the year.

From then on, the scamp moon rose and set exactly on time so he could see his sister. But, to get revenge on the world, he caused all sorts of trouble for the people living there, especially after his beloved sister moon sets each year. So, the people celebrate the scamp and sister moon at Dunkelheit Festival each year to ease his ire.

The story seemed familiar to me when I heard it. It had comforted me against the pain of recovery.

Branches crack and break to the left of me.

"Hello?" I call softly. I peer into the thicket, expecting someone to shout for me to burn off because they're taking a dump.

A figure stands, a man concealed in black armour from head to toe. It shimmers like snakeskin, and he wears a grinning wolf's mask over his face.

"Bann," I gasp. Terror surges through me. I trip backward and fall through branches into a clearing.

When I look up, it's not Bann. A different man stands in front of me, a man in ragged clothes with a scar across his face. He stares at me, his eye twitchy and his gaze locked on my chest.

I look down at myself. When I tripped, my shirt fell open, exposing my bare chest—nodes and all. I stand quickly, body tensed for a fight, but the scar-faced man just swears, spits, and stalks away.

What was that about? Thirteen asks. *Why did you trip?*

I glance around, my heart still racing, but there's no one else. I watch the man's retreating back, irritated.

"Tripped," I answer simply. "What was he doing? Taking a piss?"

Or spying on someone…

"Spying on me?"

No, on the-

"Who's there?" A voice calls out from behind me.

-the girl.

Girl? I turn around and discover a woman standing in the small clearing behind me. She's naked save for her undergirding and a schal clutched to her chest. The bastard had been peeping at her while she changed.

I'm about to put my back to her and give her some privacy when I notice something. The woman is wearing gloves, the fitted leather kind a rider or cavalryman might wear. The kind the older brother

Immaculate

always wears...

I stare at her. Stare at her brown hair that cascades past her shoulder. She's small-framed and small-boned, built like a bird. I stare at her sharp chin and straight nose, her big eyes with thick lashes, and I know in sunlight, the colour of those eyes would be a rich brown. Any other time, they will be black—a bright black like the keen eyes of a bird.

The older brother is actually an older sister, but that isn't what has my stomach in knots.

It's her skin.

Her skin is beautiful—devoid of stains, pigments, patterns, or scars.

Her skin is flawless. Immaculate.

"Freude?" The girl asks in surprise.

Why is she calling my brother's name? I stare at her, stare at her immaculately human body.

"She's not a brother," I murmur in shock.

This is what I was trying to tell you! He is a she and not a brother at all, but you said to talk about it later. You had more pressing matters to attend to, but you should have listened. A person in disguise is twenty-nine percent more likely to-

He's fixating on her disguise? She's a shattering Immaculate! "Are you burning fractured?" I snap.

I meant the words for Thirteen, but the woman's shock evaporates, bringing us both back to our senses and the realisation of her current state of undress.

"Turn around," she says, her voice deadly calm.

It's against my instincts to turn my back to an Immaculate. I scan her surroundings. Where is her retinue? Where is her koganzug user bodyguard?

But that's not right. She's travelling with a hollowbern. They were starving. She nearly died in the mangroves...

"Turn around!" she shouts, her calm shattering and her schal clutched more tightly to her chest.

I turn around quickly.

What are you doing? Thirteen hisses. *You are giving her the chance to kill you!*

'She's practically naked,' I subvocalize. 'Who kills someone while they're naked?'

Immaculate

That's what makes it so perfect. You'd never expect it.

"If the perfect time to kill someone is when they're least expecting to be killed, I'd have to expect to be killed all the time to prevent it," I whisper harshly.

Exactly. Paranoia is the most ideal safety measure.

He has a point.

As a kid, I made the mistake of thinking Immaculates were angels since they were born looking like them. I learned differently after joining the Vogt. That bloodthirsty psycho Manny was an Immaculate. An Immaculate commanded the Devils and the Vogt's other elite forces. Even Wilhelm had had no qualms turning humans into monsters up until recently.

I listen as she pulls on her clothes, flexing my hands nervously. Thirteen is right; I hate having my back exposed to an Immaculate.

'What do you think, Thirteen?' I subvocalize.

Strangle her. Less sound is better. But if you have to, a kick to the chest works, too.

I grunt in annoyance. 'Not how to kill her. Who is

she?'

I shouldn't be surprised that Thirteen assumed we'd kill her. Even if she's not an assassin, her identity is too suspicious, and Thirteen always errs on the side of caution. His paranoia kept me alive for two years as a Devil's apprentice and five years as a Devil, but I'm not with the Vogt anymore. I'm no longer a Devil.

'Which Immaculate Great House does she belong to?' I subvocalize. If Thirteen can find her registration, then I'll at least know what Great House we're dealing with.

Hm. She is unregistered.

That surprises me. 'Unregistered? That's possible?'

For Fallen, yes.

'What's that supposed to mean?'

The term comes from the Book of Revelation in a record called 'Die Bibel' in The Major Annals. Satan is cast out of Heaven and-

'Keep it brief,' I instruct. 'It sounds like she's almost done dressing.'

In short, there are two possibilities. One, she was

produced randomly just as hollowberns are and has not been adopted into a Great House. However, those who fail to adopt rarely survive long, as the existence of random Immaculate births threatens the prestige of the Great Houses; thus, they are usually quickly and rigorously addressed to suppress knowledge of them.

I try to take the information in stride, but it's a lot to take in.

'How come I've never heard of this?'

How could I with Kog Prime always around?

So, even Kog Prime wants this information suppressed.

'And the second possibility?'

Two, she was disowned by a Great House and escaped before they tattooed and enslaved her or executed her.

Enslave an Immaculate… My thoughts can't seem to get beyond that idea, but Thirteen just keeps on talking.

Though, I suppose there is the possibility that she was born in a country that does not register Immaculates.

'But if she was born in another country, what's she doing fleeing from the Reichland? Why not go back to her country?'

Considering the number of potential scenarios, I am unable to give you an answer.

'What do you mean?'

In other words, use your imagination. I don't have one.

Damn sulky machine, but I suppose he has a point. My situation is complicated enough, how is Thirteen supposed to guess hers?

"You can turn back around," the woman says. She sounds calmer now.

I face her. She's dressed in a clean set of trousers and a collarless button-up. Suspenders stretch over her shoulders. No hint of a woman's curves. She must bind her chest and pad her waist. With the Dustlands' heat, I don't envy her.

She twists her dark hair into a knot atop her head, skewering it with a hair clasp. Then she pulls a flat cap over all of it. Last, she slips on her half-cloak and wraps her schal around her neck. She looks like the young man I met once again.

"Why do you disguise yourself as a boy?" I ask.

Who sent you? What do you want? What are you planning? Why is your schal that colour of blue?

I ignore Thirteen. This situation is complicated enough without him turning it into one of the theatrical dramas he likes.

"It's just me and Mikael," she answers carefully. "Being a woman is a liability out here. It's safer if people believe I'm a boy."

I think of the murdered merchant couple and their kidnapped daughter. She's not wrong.

"How old are you?" I try to sound casual as I try to figure out her situation—as I try to gauge the threat.

"Nineteen," she answers.

"Where's home?"

"Not here." She shrugs, but it's forced. Her guard is up, too.

"What's an Immaculate doing travelling with a hollowbern?"

She tenses, but it seems like she was expecting the question. "He's my brother."

Liar. I let my casual demeanour fall.

"Right," I snort derisively. "I lived around the Great Houses. There's no way in hell that the same two parents gave birth to an Immaculate and a hollowbern and lived. More like you picked him up somewhere and are using him as a disguise. That way everyone assumes you're both hollowberns."

Sounds logical, Thirteen says approvingly.

"That's not what I'm doing," the woman argues. "We-"

She stops herself and glances around anxiously, like she's afraid someone might overhear. Bites her bottom lip, hesitating.

Finally, she continues quietly. "We have the same father," she says, "but I grew up outside of the home after my mother died. Mikael was born several years after I left and is registered under our housekeeper... But he's still my brother!"

Fascinating! The boy is the result of an affair. That

would explain why they were being followed.

Yes, it would. Even without the genocide, these siblings would have had to flee the Reichland. An Immaculate whose blood sibling is a hollowbern... If she's telling the truth, both the Arkist Church and the Immaculate Great Houses would want them dead.

My heart sinks into my stomach.

Trouble. Whether she's telling the truth or not, it all spells trouble, and I have enough of that on my own. I can't afford more. The last time I took on this kind of trouble, I failed and people died because of it.

"My brother and I need to reach Rettung. Will you take us there?" she asks me.

"No." I take a step back, a step away from her.

"I can pay you." Her expression looks hopeful.

"I don't need money." I take another step back.

She looks down, thinking. Her hands fidget, touching her pockets, her head, her hat—desperately searching. She looks up suddenly, hope rekindled in her face.

"Korrectives," she blurts. "You don't have any, I

checked. I can provide you with them until we reach Rettung."

Korrectives, Leviatan! Thirteen cheers.

She recognised my symptoms, knows I need the korrectives to prevent blood rot. No surprise, I guess, since she has enough medical knowledge and skills to perform surgery.

"Why do you even want my help?" I ask not for a reason to agree but to find a way to dissuade her.

"You taught me where to find eggs, and you risked your life to save mine." She smiles at me, a wan, desperate little smile. "We can help each other."

Korrectives would be nice, Thirteen says. *Let's work with her!*

Her naivety twists in my gut. She's going to get herself killed. "Or I could just kill you and take the korrectives," I reply.

Or that... Thirteen agrees, totally serious.

"Maybe I saw your pack of supplies and did all of this to get close to you? Maybe I'll live off your korrectives and then sell you and your brother as soon as we reach Rettung?"

Oh! Thirteen exclaims. *Now your previous behaviour makes sense. I apologize for questioning you!*

Ruthless machine. He can't distinguish between cruelty and wisdom—they're both logic to him.

The girl's smile withers, realizing her mistake. Realizing too, how little she knows about me.

"Piece of advice," I tell her, "if you want to reach Rettung alive, trust no one but yourself." I turn away from her and head back the way I came, but her voice stops me from leaving the clearing.

"Please help us," she says quietly.

She's desperate. She's pleading. She's begging. But I'm a bastard, and I have two letters and too many secrets already. She needs to let me go. I need to convince her to let me go.

"Why would I help you?" I reply, arrogance curdling my words. "You're worthless to me."

She has the korrectives, Thirteen argues.

"You're foolish," I continue, trying to ignore him.

She has medical training, Thirteen interjects.

He doesn't get it. He doesn't understand how dangerous it would be to stay with them.

"Weak," I tell her. Tell Thirteen too.

She saved you from the golem.

So what if she saved me? I saved her too. "And you're travelling with a hollowbern. Hollowberns bring bad luck. Everyone knows that."

You thought they were both hollowberns before, and it didn't bother you. Honestly, now you're nit-picking. She offered you korrectives and we need korrectives. The least you could do is pretend to help them out, get the korrectives, and then dump them.

Dump them. Take what you need and leave. I clench my fists until my knuckles pop. Do to them what was done to me…

"I'm not taking a little girl and her gods-damned cur to Rettung!"

I yell at Thirteen, eyes on the moonlight and shadows in front of me. I'm so tired of him questioning every decision I make. He just doesn't get it—doesn't understand what it's like wanting to do right, but also wanting to live, and never having those two things coincide.

Something hits me in the head and nearly knocks me to my knees, knocks me out of my thoughts. I raise my eyes to the Immaculate as she digs out a fist-sized stone from the sand and chucks it at me. For as small as she is, I never would have thought she could throw a stone that size so far and hard.

"You can't say that," she yells.

I dodge the stone and the next that sails in behind it. She's a bird, an angry little bird. Lost her temper and is pitching a fit.

I wasn't talking to her, but now I know her sore spot. Gods forgive me for what I'm about to say.

"What?" I sneer. "You don't want me to call you a little girl? Fine. You're a shattering mascot for genocide, and that brother of yours is one of the bloody curs they're killing."

"Shut up!" she screams.

I dodge another stone.

Leviatan, it appears the woman is attempting to assassinate you. I strongly urge you to kill her now and take her korrectives.

"She's not trying to kill me," I retort.

The next one is over my head, but the next hits me in the thigh, a furious blow. She'd peck my eyes out if I let her. The next hits near my wound, and I grunt in pain.

Maim you. She is definitely trying to maim you, which is basically the same thing.

Time for the finishing blow—she needs to be scared of me for us to finish this.

I stalk toward her, accepting the blows as she throws more stones. When I reach her she raises an arm, ready to let another stone fly at point-blank range. I grip her wrist. She freezes, eyes wide in surprise, startled out of her blind fury.

"Let go of me." She tries to jerk her arm away, but my hold is firm. She retaliates, kicks me hard in the shin with the toe of her boot. It hurts worse than getting sideswiped by that damnable golem. I swear and push her away.

She stumbles and falls into the stones and dirt, crying out and cupping her hand. A stone tore through one of her gloves. I don't see any blood, but she cradles the hand against her chest, glaring at me. There's fear in the glare too, but her expression hardens with bitterness and cold anger.

"Don't insult my brother that way," she hisses. "He's as much a human being as you."

She uses a Manual word, 'menschlik,' for 'human being.' In Manual, it means more than just 'human being,' more than the biological attributes of Homo sapiens. It's a collective identity, a sense of belonging. A word that will never be mine.

She was telling the truth, I realise. She isn't using him as a disguise. They are siblings—the kind I wish I'd had. She loves him. She fights for him. She stays with him. A part of me is drawn to her because of that.

But I recover my composure and scoff at the irony of her comment. He's as human as I am, is he? She wouldn't say that if she knew what kind of creature she was saying that to.

"And what if I don't consider myself to be *menschlik*?" I ask.

"Then he's better off than you."

I smile bitterly. "True enough."

I slip my hands into my pockets, give her a little bow, and speak in clipped phrases. "With that said, I doubt I could be of much use to you. Thank you for the medical assistance."

I go back to camp and gather my belongings. The boy still hugs his overlarge pack, but his breathing tells me he's likely awake. Maybe he's making sure I don't steal their stuff before I go? If so, there's hope for his sister. This brother of hers, he's like the boy I used to be—the boy I don't have the courage to act like anymore. I hope things turn out better for him than they did for me.

I wrap Freude's red schal around my throat, swing Wilhelm's satchel over my shoulder, and turn my back on their camp.

I walk away.

Immaculate

And that's okay. Because now, everything is back to how it was before I met them. It's as if nothing happened. Nothing has changed. Things are as they should be—as I want them to be.

At least, that's what I tell myself as I leave them behind.

Chapter 22: Monster

The day before Freude left. Nine years ago.

"Is it time?" I shouted, perched at the edge of Keim's bed in only my underwear. The sister moon was already past full on the horizon and the sun high in the sky, but it was just too scorching hot to wear clothes.

In other places, the fallow season meant a cool down. Here, it meant it was too shattering hot for even trees to move, and then a Great Storm would roll in and hit us over the head with ice for a week. Normally, I slept the afternoons away with the rest of the Dustlands, but today wasn't any normal day. Today was the first day of the Dunkelheit Festival and our last day with Freude.

Monster

"Keim, is it time yet? Can we go?" I shouted again.

Keim rolled over, groaning, and pulled his blankets over his head, unveiling his own bare, and surprisingly hairy, legs. The thick, new growth had sprung up in only the last few months. I fought the urge to pinch some and give it a good, hard yank. That'd get him out of bed, but it'd also earn me a beating. Instead, I hopped off the bed and opened his shutters.

Afternoon sunlight spilled into the room, fell over the dishevelled bed and chaos of bookshelves. On his nightstand, lay a thick volume with a dirty sock wedged into it to hold his place, but the floor was strikingly clean because when Mum complained about Keim's room, he shoved everything under his bed. Dry clothes, dust, trash—a messy life was nothing to him.

But then there was his work bench, the sturdy desk I envied stationed beneath his window where he could get the best natural light: screws sorted by size in bins, scrap metal in a box, and tools hung on a board. He surrendered everything to chaos save this. He might neglect his chores, his family, his health, but anything having to do with reengineering was cared for with meticulous ardour.

That was Keim. He had his dream—everything else could go to hell.

"Keim! Is it time for the festival?" I shook his shoulder insistently.

He swatted me away. "Go ask Ehren," he grumbled.

Ehren? What kind of fool did he take me for? I wasn't looking to die.

Keim groaned and turned over.

Looked like he was a lost cause too. But Mum was in with a patient, and Da was doing morning chores. That left Freude. I just had to hunt him down.

I hopped down from Keim's bed and left the room. The wood floors creaked as I trotted back to my bedroom. Would Freude be in the barn with Da? Helping Mum? Maybe he'd be in the pasture or the urvogel hutch or with Knopse...

Fishing, I decided. With the festival this afternoon and him leaving for the Vogt tomorrow, he'd be down at the crick fishing one last time.

I struggled into some trousers and pulled on a shirt as I stumbled out the backdoor barefooted. I might regret leaving off my shoes in an hour or two, but for now, the sand and stones might as well be carpet under my calloused feet.

I was right. Freude lay in the brittle grass beside the crick, a fishing rod propped with stones beside him. He'd folded his arms behind his head and pinched a green strauch shoot between his teeth.

He still looked weird to me without his Dustlander braids. He'd hacked them off himself last night because Mum refused to cut them for him. Keim cleaned up the hack job with one of his gadgets. Now, Freude's red braids and beads had given way to a carpet of red velvet. Made his enlistment with the Vogt's military that much more real.

I squatted down beside his head, folded my arms over my knees. "Is it time, yet?"

Freude squinted at me, barely opening his eyes. He closed them again and smiled. "That excited for the festival, are you?"

Was I? The buzzing sensation in my belly might have been excitement, or just anxiety. There'd be a lot of people at the festival tonight. Lots of faces and eyes and talking... My mouth went dry. "Sort of. Is the festival fun?"

Freude sat up, studied me. "Mum is finally letting you go instead of making you stay home with her. You ought to be excited." He grinned slyly. "Is there anyone you're looking forward to seeing? Maybe someone you have in mind for the ribbon dance?"

I blushed. "No."

Freude's smile widened. "Bluhen will be sorry to hear that."

Bluhen, Knopse's sister. I grimaced, my blush deepening. "She'd be the last person I'd ask."

I wasn't like Freude. Freude talked with everyone so easily. By the time he'd been my age, he'd already settled his relationship with Knopse, our neighbour's daughter. He'd been ten years old and dead-set on taking care of her forever, and Knopse was the same way. Even with Freude reporting to the Vogt, she'd be here waiting when he got home. That's just the way they were.

I liked Knopse. She'd make a good sister. She could sit beside me and say nothing for hours, but her little sister was of another nature. Bluhen had been chasing me around ever since I can remember, telling me I'd already promised to marry her. Not that I recalled, but that didn't stop her from telling everyone else. Stupid girl.

Just thinking about Bluhen made me shudder. "Do I have to go?"

Freude laughed. "You know, there's more to life than animals, action figures, and drawing. Getting out and interacting with real people would do you some good."

"Mum says using my imagination is good for my brain."

"And she's right, but what good is a healthy brain if you don't use it for anything else?"

"I use it for school."

"And what is school good for?"

"To learn to do stuff. And get a job." Were there any jobs that let me draw all day without ever seeing another person?

Freude shook his head with a smile, like he could hear my thoughts. "If you don't ever talk to real people, why would you need to do stuff or get a job? You could live on the farm, take care of the animals, be totally self-reliant, and never see a soul for the rest of your life."

"Could I really?"

Freude laughed and ruffled my hair. "That wasn't supposed to sound like an ideal lifestyle. People need people. Would a person know if they became something else, like a monster, if there was no one else around them?"

I perked up. "Like in that book we read at school? With the scientist and the dead body he brings to life and stuff?"

Freude scoffed. "Even Frankenstein's monster wanted a companion. Promise me you'll try to make friends?"

Did everyone need someone then? Who did I need? Mum, for sure. Who else would take care of me when I was sick, or take time to teach me stuff, or hug me when I was sad?

"Maybe someday I'll need someone," I answered thoughtfully. I offered my pinkie to make a promise. Freude hooked it with his, and we pressed our thumbs together to seal it.

"But not Bluhen," I rushed to clarify.

Freude burst into a laugh. "Fine, not Bluhen."

Chapter 23: To Not Turn Away

∞

Papa, I believe a person's will is in their
hands, and their heart is in their eyes.
If I had let you cover my eyes, what would
that have made me?

∞

I wake in the early morning shivering, sweat drenching my hair and shirt, body aching. A headache hammers behind my eyes, a hangover from hell. Every touch, even just my rough blanket, grates on my skin, and sitting up sends knifing pain through my side—the side effects of surgery on a wasting body.

The dream-like memory lingers in my mind. It's the first memory that took place before Freude left. There's a feeling to it—a warm glow—that my mind tries to hold onto only to have it fall to pieces. It tells me my home wasn't always wretched.

I reach for my pack and notice my sketchpad open beside it. When was I drawing? What was I drawing? I drag it over. On the open page is a face neither pretty nor ugly, all sharp lines, petite features, and bird-bright black eyes.

You were not... yourself last night, Thirteen says. It's not often the AI lacks words to express himself.

"I was drunk." I throw the sketchpad closed.

A few minutes of digging and I retrieve fever reducers from my med kit only to discover my canteen empty. I swallow the painkillers dry and chase the bitterness with a sap chew. My stomach hates me for it. I lay back down, feeling pain and exhaustion deep in my bones. It feels like my body is giving up.

"Just get me to Rettung," I murmur. "Let me complete this last task. You can rest after that."

Who? Me? Thirteen asks, sounding confused.

"Nothing. Anything to report from last night?"

A solitary person approached camp not long after the fire burned down. They stayed downwind so I could not run a scent analysis.

"Stayed downwind, huh? Do you think it's coincidence?" Or is it someone that knows what I am?

I voice the first question but only think the second. I don't want to say it out loud. Feels like bad luck. My mind shies away from thoughts of the anzug users from the train two days ago and Bann.

I've compiled a list of suspects drawn from recent events. Aside from those anzug users from the train and Bann—suspects even an idiot would consider—

I try not to resent that statement.

I also included the Immaculate woman, her brother, the pervert you caught last night and fought with two days ago, the resistance fighters who bombed the train, the child who gave you the feather, the railroad supervisor you punched three days ago, a guy who gave you a funny look five days ago, the members of your crew-

"Hold it. You're basically listing anyone I made eye

contact with in the last week."

Not basically. I am. Eye contact means they noticed us. Noticing us is a bad thing.

Huh. He's not wrong. When it comes to meeting new faces, once is coincidence; twice is fate; three times is intentional.

"Fine," I reply. "Let me know if we run into anyone on that list again."

Dawn paints the skyline blue and the sister moon sits above it, an early morning first quarter moon. I study the fading stars, procrastinating. I don't want to see the sand, the stunted trees, or the desperate people.

Sperlings screech in the strauch tree behind me. The little reptilian birds erupt into furious chatter with first light. Now, it's truly morning. I sigh and reach for my satchel, retrieving the letter from Wilhelm's daughter.

My eyes rove the lines of looping script. She has good handwriting. I trace an old stain on the paper, a dark circle smudging the ink. She cried as she wrote it but kept her letters neat regardless.

Hollowberns and beatings, innocence and rage, a

father and his daughter—those are the things she wrote about, but what was she thinking as she wrote them? Was she saying goodbye? Was she trying to change her father? Was she trying to hold onto him?

"All I could do for him was watch," she says. "All I had to offer was to not turn away." I touch those words, my dirty fingers brushing across them.

Her tone implies watching is a small thing, but it's not. Refusing to turn away from a stranger's pain is no small thing, and to do it while powerless to help? The idea frightens me. I'm the kind of person who doesn't want to bring his eyes down from the stars and face his own problems, least of all someone else's. Every time I try, I make things worse.

I put the letter away and walk over to the area Thirteen indicates was where the suspect stood during the night. There aren't many traces left, just a few broken branches. The wind scattered any prints and the scent has already dissipated. There's nothing to be done but pack and move on, so that's what I do.

I walk the meandering path down the bluff toward

the well, listening to the river rushing nearby. Sperling birds continue to curse at each other. They'll quiet once the dark hour begins, confused into roosting.

The solar eclipses that occur daily are called the "dark hours," and they bring eerie silences and gloom to the daylight hours. My mother told me that in the Endonine language, the word for dark hour translates to "little death."

In planting season, there are two dark hours. The first dark hour is when the sun rises and moves behind the scamp moon as it sets. The second dark hour occurs only half the year, when the sun passes behind the sister moon. During Dunkelheit Festival, the first and second dark hours happen at the same time, and then the sister moon sets.

Even though the first dark hour happens every day, today, I decide to stop and watch it—not the eclipse, but the land. As I stand on a dune and look over the river, a shadow passes over the landscape, and the sun dims.

No, not dims. The little death is not light dimming—

the little death is when light hides itself.

'He's as much a human being as you,' the Immaculate woman said. I touch the bruises where she beat me last night. I smile sadly, feeling the ache of my swollen lip. She beat me like she would have beaten anyone. Despite fear and without hesitation, she treated me the same way she would treat anyone—as someone human.

The sun moves and the world brightens again. I move on.

Around a bend in the trail, I run into a crowd of bystanders. Everyone's attention is on a short and stout woman and her two grown sons. The woman is a Lowly with two short horns protruding from her chin that she keeps filed flat. Her sons have the same. They loom over a hollowbern youth who kneels in the dirt in front of them.

More people mill about behind the crowd in the shade off the trail, men with weathered faces and carefully blank expressions. They carry heavily laden packs, not survival gear. Cargo porters. Their gazes flit to the woman and away, watching the goings-on but trying not to. She must be their boss.

"Filthy cur," the merchant woman says. She spits at the boy. "I don't employ creatures like you. Don't dare ask again."

I pass through the crowd. The youth looks at me as I come abreast of them. Grey eyes and brown hair. No Lowly features. He'd look as lovely as any Immaculate save for the raised black stains that spread like roots across his face.

Not even old enough for facial hair, but he's got the eyes of a weary old man. Too tired to hate.

The merchant woman keeps railing, spit flying from her lips. "You're like leeches, take jobs away from good, worthy folks. Suck the life out of our communities. Now you're flooding Rettung like a plague."

Cur. Communities. Life. Plague. My mind plucks the words from her tirade and rolls them around like marbles, sensing the weight of them.

"I'll take less pay," the boy says. "Or no pay at all as

long as I get food."

The porters react immediately, shouting at the boy and throwing things at him. He rolls to his side and covers his head. It's hard to watch, and it makes me wonder—what's worse, someone who watches and does nothing, or someone who doesn't watch at all?

The merchant woman laughs in a short, harsh burst. "If I cared about that, then all my porters would be curs." She spits again. "Like I said, leeches."

Murmurs of assent. Quick, low conversations. A ripple of tension.

I stare at my boots and walk on, intent on ignoring the spectacle, but someone steps in front of me. I look up and discover a familiar face—a woman wearing men's clothes, her brown hair hidden in a flat cap, gloves covering her hands and forearms, and her schal wrapped so high it covers half her face. She looks at me, black eyes cold. Then she looks past me, and I can't help but feel a prick of shame.

Leviatan, we have come into contact again with a suspect.

To Not Turn Away

Twice is fate. Is it a good or bad one?

She pushes past me, knocking her shoulder into mine. My eyes follow her, and I can't help turning around as she passes.

Small as she is, she still inserts herself between the merchant woman's sons and the hollowbern. The two sons tower over her. They seem perplexed by the small, angry person before them.

Their mother pushes between the two men and gets right up in the Immaculate's face, something she would never dared do if she knew the girl's blood status.

But the Immaculate says nothing, just glares at the merchants and cargo porters. The black-brown of her bird-bright eyes glitter like deep water, dark and disturbing.

She's that angry little bird again, a huge temper in a tiny body. She's too small to hurt them, but the way she stares down the merchant and the two sons makes enough of an impression that the porters and bystanders fall silent.

As I watch her, I hear her words again from last

night: 'He's as much a human being as you.'

Her words remind me of the letter from Wilhelm's daughter. I think Wilhelm's daughter would like her, this fierce little bird.

Yes, Little Bird. That is what Wilhelm's daughter would call her. That's what we could call her.

"What?" The merchant woman snaps at Little Bird, folding her thick arms over her chest. When she remains silent, the merchant lifts her chin. "What! Are you a cur lover? If you have something to say, say it."

Will she show them she's an Immaculate? Thirteen asks. He sounds both excited and perplexed.

'Only a fool would,' I answer back, but I wonder the same. If Little Bird loses her temper like last night and reveals herself as an Immaculate, she could easily put this merchant and her sons in their places. It would seem like the easiest solution to a stupid person.

Agreed. It would be a short term gain with long term consequences.

Huh. Thirteen and I actually agree on something. That's a rarity.

To Not Turn Away

Fortunately, Little Bird isn't the fool I feared she was. She holds her temper and stands in stony silence, glaring. Wind rattles in the strauch needles and snaps at her clothes and pack.

Then the merchant woman raises her hand and slaps Little Bird across the face.

Anger grips me. I step toward them but force myself to stop. This has nothing to do with me. She has nothing to do with me.

That's what I tell myself, but I'm not convinced.

Some of the other bystanders murmur in distaste. The girl hasn't said or done anything, was it necessary to hit her? Other bystanders hoot and holler, ready for the show to escalate. These ones likely have ulterior motives for watching.

Leviatan, your heartrate has elevated significantly in the last few seconds, Thirteen informs me. *According to my analysis in corroboration with the current situation, you are apparently angry. Taking into account last night's events, I have concluded that you would like to hit the rock-throwing woman as well. But I encourage you to release your frustration through healthier outlets, like jogging or meditation.*

"Idiot," I mutter in response.

Throwing pottery seems to yield positive results as well.

Over three thousand survey questions and this is the result. Brilliant.

Another suspect on my list is incoming, Thirteen says.

The little brother darts past me, face twisted with fury. Even an idiot would know he's headed for trouble. I grab him by the arm, wrap my hand across his mouth, and restrain his head against my shoulder.

"If you don't want to get her killed, stay out of it," I hiss.

He bites me, sinking his teeth into my hand, but I endure the pain rather than let go.

His sister has a broad definition of human, it seems, Thirteen comments.

Again, we agree on something, but that's something I like about her.

To Not Turn Away

Little Bird, a red handprint standing out on her cheek, turns back to the merchant and her sons and continues to stare them down. The merchant lifts her chin in stubbornness, but she keeps glancing at the people watching.

She's losing her nerve, I realise. It's one thing to bully a hollowbern. It's another to bully someone who hasn't said a word. Not only that, she knows if the situation escalates, some people will use the chaos to steal her merchandise.

It's a stalemate, and she knows it.

"May the Arkists take you and good riddance," the merchant woman snarls. Then she turns her back on Little Bird and the hollowbern on the ground. Her sons follow and then all the porters. Soon, everyone is bustling and moving out.

Little Bird won. I feel the tension in my shoulders release. I'm surprised how satisfied I feel from her victory. All she did was watch and that was enough.

I release the boy, shoving him into the crowd, and wipe blood from my hand. I watch him disappear into the throng. After everything, the brat doesn't even approach his sister.

The crowd clears, leaving the hollowbern youth alone on the ground. He curls up in the dirt, his arms over his head like he's expecting a blow any minute. I take out my bag of strauch chews and drop it beside him. He peeks out from beneath his arms.

"Make them last," I say and walk away. I don't know if he takes them or not. It doesn't matter. At least I did something. If I hadn't, I don't think I could look the little bird woman in the eye again.

Look her in the eye?

That's when I realise I'm looking for her, and at that moment of realisation, I find her, a slim figure in men's clothes, a flat cap, and gloves moving quickly down the road.

To not turn away, does it make a difference? I wonder. My hand rests on Wilhelm's satchel where the letters are hidden.

What's worse, someone who watches and does nothing, or someone who doesn't bother to watch at all?

To Not Turn Away

My brothers come to mind—Freude and his schal, Ehren and his wooden soldiers, and Keim with his stuffed elephant. Back then, they left gifts for apologies when what I really needed was for them to not turn away.

Wilhelm's daughter said, 'Only a devil lives with their eyes closed.'

Yes, not turning away means something, I realise. It means if I don't help this Immaculate woman and her brother, I will never deliver Wilhelm's letter. There would be no point. I would still be the devil I've always been.

Chapter 24: What Is Owed

∞

Only a devil lives with their eyes closed.

∞

I freeze in motionless surprise in the middle of the trail, my feet refusing to move farther. A refugee couple forces past me with their cart, knocking me to the side of the road.

Leviatan, Thirteen asks, w*hat is your current status?*

My current status? Insane. Definitely insane. Only a crazy person puts their life and freedom on the line for someone who beat him with rocks the night before and a kid who bit him.

"We're going after her," I reply, and I start to run.

Are you still angry because she hit you with rocks?

What Is Owed

Regardless, I strongly encourage you not to kill her, Thirteen says with utmost seriousness, *unless you plan to take her korrectives, too.*

"Not to hurt her," I reply. "To accept her offer."

We're accepting her offer? Hurray!

"Hurray?" I ask in surprised. "I thought you suspected her of being an assassin?"

I do suspect it, but immediate risks should be mitigated before dealing with more abstract probabilities. It's a logic thing—you wouldn't get it.

The jab is typical of Thirteen, but this one echoes of Perri's personality. A knot forms in my throat. It's been awhile since I allowed myself to think of her.

Little Bird is hard to follow. She is smaller than many of the other refugees, one moving body among many. Thirteen helps, but I have to move quickly to keep up, causing my wound to ache deeply.

I dodge between people, craning my neck to spot her flat cap and schal or her half-length cloak and gloves. I glimpse her as she takes a path away from the main road.

I walk swiftly along the edge of the road, skirting carts of belongings and cargo porters, trying to keep her in my sights. I take the same side trail she did and pick up my speed. It's a rugged path, more like an animal track than a trail. It takes a sharp turn and I run, worried now that Little Bird is out of sight. Afraid I might lose her. Afraid she might leave me behind.

I round the bend.

The little bird woman stands in the middle of the path, hands on her hips, waiting for me. I grind to a halt, stopping so hard that my boots skid, sending up a cloud of dust.

Three times is intentional.

She glares at me. "Why are you following me?"

I clear my throat, caught off guard. "I wasn't," I lie.

You weren't? Thirteen asks, confused. *I thought you said-*

"Yes, you were," she argues. "You've been following me since I got slapped."

I spoke in Common and she answered back in Narrisch. She understands more Common than I realised. The handprint stands out on her Immaculate skin, violently red, and her cheek has begun to swell.

"Does it hurt?" I ask, like an idiot.

She folds her arms across her chest and scowls, a finger tapping her arm in annoyance.

I think it hurts, Thirteen offers helpfully.

"Are you here for the immune korrectives? Now is your chance to take them. There is no one else around," she says bitterly.

Is that an offer to take them?

She's right. I could take them from her with no problem right now. Not even her brother is here. But that's not why I came.

"I want to accept your offer-" I reply.

To take the korrectives?

"-to escort you to Rettung."

Oh.

Her eyebrows rise sceptically. "What if this 'little girl and her gods-damned cur'"—she quotes my words bitingly—"aren't offering that deal anymore?"

You'll just take the korrectives, right? Thirteen asks

hopefully.

I pause to stop myself from snapping at Thirteen in front of her, but she takes it as hesitation. Something like disappointment crosses her face, and she starts to turn away from me.

"I'll give it anyway," I blurt. "My help."

She turns back to me, seeming surprised. "What?"

Yeah! What? Thirteen echoes. *How can we help without korrectives? Stupid, so stupid...*

I ignore Thirteen and take a deep breath. "Look, I don't like people, and I don't trust Immaculates." She looks surprised. She probably expected me to say hollowberns. "But you saved my life twice yesterday. I owe you, and I acknowledge that. So, I'll get you and your brother to Rettung, but..."

Her expression closes with suspicion. "But?" she asks.

"But I can't escort you all the way without korrectives."

"Well said," she scoffs. "You've neatly wrapped your greed in honour."

Oh, I like that adage. Thirteen exclaims. *She will be great at answering survey questions. Fine, I withdraw my objections as long as you ask her my survey questions.*

So, Thirteen prioritizes his survey questions over survival? Where's the logic in that?

Little Bird takes three brisk steps forward so she's standing directly in front of me, forcing my full attention on her. She looks up, studying my face with her eyes narrowed in suspicion.

I look back nervously, forcing myself to stand in place. She grabs Freude's schal that's wrapped around my neck and jerks my head down until our faces are level. I swallow hard, my throat dry. I only ever let Perri get this close to me before.

Without warning, Little Bird drives the toe of her boot into my shin like a hammer. I yelp and lose my balance, going down to one knee. I stand again quickly, my leg throbbing.

Leviatan, according to your vitals, that was painful.

"Yeah…" I grunt.

"That's for being so mean last night," she snaps. Then she kicks me in the other shin. I wince, more prepared this time. "And that's for leaving."

Oh, I like her, Thirteen exclaims gleefully. *If we're going to die doing this letter delivery quest at least it has just become more interesting!*

The woman releases Freude's schal and lets me recover before speaking again. She slips her gloved hands into her trouser pockets.

"I normally give people only one chance," she says, looking at the horizon and not me. "There are a lot of things I can forgive, but not leaving. If you do what you did last night again, I'll never forgive you."

She's a little silly, isn't she? If you leave, you'll never see each other again. How is hating you any sort of punishment? She'd be better off holding the korrectives hostage.

It seems this Immaculate already knows me better in just forty-eight hours than Thirteen who's had seven years and 3,221 questions to get to know me. She doesn't need to hold the korrectives hostage; she's grabbed hold of my guilt instead.

She turns to give me a discerning look. Then she raises one gloved hand and forms a fist save for the pinkie and offers it to me. "Promise you'll get us to Rettung. Promise you'll stay that long."

I notice it's the glove that tore when she fell last night. She's already stitched it up neat and tidy. I hook her pinkie with mine and we press our thumbs together to seal it, just like I did as a kid.

"Promise," I answer, feeling the ominous weight of that word.

She nods, dropping my hand and walking past me in the direction we came from. Makes me wonder why she came here in the first place. To test me? I thought her simple, but then, I've never known a simple Immaculate.

"My name is Sara, by the way," she says over her shoulder. "My brother's is Mikael. He doesn't talk to strangers though, and he doesn't like when they talk to me…"

She continues speaking as I let my thoughts wander.

Sara. The name suits her. According to The Annals, 'Sara' means 'princess' in one of the lost origin languages, but I like Little Bird better.

"Are you coming or not, Freude?" Sara calls, interrupting herself.

Hearing the name unsettles me. I forgot that is the name I gave her yesterday. I perform a mock bow to conceal my pause and motion her onward with a flourish. It works. She glares at me and marches ahead.

Leiden, why did you change your mind about helping her? Thirteen asks.

I'm surprised to hear Thirteen use my given name. I don't think he has before. So, for once, I give him an honest answer.

"A long time ago, my brother told me people need people. He said that without others, we become monsters. So, I promised him I would try to make friends. Wilhelm's daughter says something similar in her letter."

So this is part of your initiative to become something other than a Devil?

"Yes."

To become more human even though it is so very hard?

"Yes."

Oh, okay.

That's all Thirteen says. He talks the most when it matters least and talks the least when I actually want to hear what he has to say.

I shrug, a little embarrassed. "I figured I'd try it out. Besides, we need the korrectives, right?"

And if it goes badly, we can just leave, Thirteen adds.

Right. Leave. My hand still tingles where it touched hers to make our promise.

I shake off the clinging web of thoughts and feelings and follow the little bird woman named Sara. Wilhelm's satchel bounces against my hip, a sketchbook, wood carvings, a Devil's mask and plague blade, and two letters safely nestled inside.

The story continues in

All Light and Darkness,

Volume 2

Book One of *The Books of Leiden* series

Glossary

Pronunciations are spelled phonetically.
/ái/ is pronounced like the I-sound in "bye".

People

- **Leiden (L/ái/-den) Talson (Tall-son)** – tall and
skinny, bronze skin, iridescent blue hair and gold
eyes – the main character; Bann brought him to the
Vogt when he was eleven and severely injured; to
save his life, Bann had him receive the koganzug
installation surgery; Leiden cannot remember
anything that happened before the surgery; he
became a Devil (Agent Leviatan) to repay his life-
debt to Bann; eighteen years old

- **Thirteen** – Leiden's kognitive auxiliary; Thirteen
manages Leiden's koganzug, manipulating the
biomechs as needed, and maintains a local archive
of data for Leiden's use; Thirteen is supposed to
synchronize with Kog Prime regularly to report on
Leiden and to homogenize Thirteen's personality,
but synching doesn't work on Thirteen's personality

- **Sara** – petite, long brown hair, black eyes with
pronounced epicanthal folds – a refugee Leiden
meets while traveling to Rettung; Sara is traveling
incognito with her younger half-brother Mikael;
Leiden thinks Sara is a hollowbern man when he

349

first meets her and discovers later that she is an Immaculate woman; Leiden agrees to help Sara and Mikael reach Rettung in exchange for korrectives; nineteen years old

- **Mikael (Mee-k/ái/-el)** – skinny and tan, black hair, icy blue monolid eyes – Sara's younger half-brother, supposedly the child of their father and their housekeeper; Mikael is a hollowbern with stains on his back and chest; Mikael is very protective of his sister and antagonistic toward strangers; he especially dislikes Leiden; ten years old

- **Typ (Tip)** – short and muscled, brown and green pigmented skin, scar spanning his face, ruining one eye – a Lowly refugee Leiden meets after the train explosion; Typ acts suspiciously so Leiden chases him; Typ was robbing the bodies of a family of merchants attacked by slavers

- **Wilhelm's daughter** – the author of the letter Leiden reads frequently given to him by Wilhelm along with a letter Wilhelm wrote to his daughter; Leiden agreed to deliver Wilhelm's letter to his daughter in hopes of receiving help removing his koganzug in return; quotes from the letter Wilhelm's daughter wrote are featured as epigraphs in this novel

- **Dr. Reuben Wilhelm** – a Vogt scientist that changed sides and worked for the Guild Coalition Government and the Neo-Arkists; Leiden was supposed to assassinate him but made a deal with him instead; Leiden agreed to help him escape in exchange for help removing his koganzug; later, Leiden agreed to deliver a letter to Wilhelm's daughter instead

- **Dr. Mia Kroff** – a scientist that worked with Dr. Reuben Wilhelm in the hidden laboratory in Bergverk

- **Clara Neuseman (Noos-man)** – the leader of the Neo-Arkist religious movement within the Arkist Church; she arranged an alliance with the Vogt and took over as the new Noah of the Arkist Church after the former Noah was killed at Bergverk; she instigated the hollowbern cleansing in the Reichland

- **Jesebel** – the leader of the acrobat terrorist attack that takes place at the Peace Banquet at Bergverk

- **Sagrim** – Jesebel's right hand person and the 'white bird' acrobat that attacks Leiden at the Peace Banquet

- **Knopse (Kin-nohp-seh)** – Freude's girlfriend from Leiden's childhood memories

- **Bluhen (Bloo-hen)** – Knopse's little sister from Leiden's childhood memories; she had a crush on Leiden

Talson (Tall-son) Family

- **Mal (Maal)** – Leiden's "Da"

Glossary

- **Ella (El-luh)** - Leiden's "Mum"; the town doctor and formerly a citizen of the Reichland

- **Freude (Froyd-duh)** – Leiden's eldest brother who joins the Vogt military to protect his younger brothers from the draft; eighteen years old when he leaves

- **Ehren (Ehr-ruhn)** – Leiden's second eldest brother who idolizes Freude but fights violently with his younger brothers; fifteen years old when Freude leaves

- **Keim (K/ái/m)** – Leiden's third eldest brother who loves relics and re-engineering; thirteen years old when Freude leaves

- **Leiden (L/ái/-den)** – the main character and the youngest in the family; almost nine years old when Freude leaves

Devils

- **Leviatan (Lev-v/ái/-uh-tan)** – the Devil of Envy; Leiden's call-sign

- **Bann (Baan)** – from the call-sign **Wolfsbann (Wolfs-baan)**; the Captain of the Devils and Leiden's mentor; he brought Leiden to the Vogt to save his life; he did not want Leiden to become a Devil

- **Perri** – from the call-sign **Perchta (Perch-tuh)**; a Devil working in reconnaissance; Leiden's close friend and fellow apprentice under Bann

- **Manny (Man-nee)** – from the call-sign **Mammon**, the Devil of Greed; a specialist in interrogation and torture; Bann rival and Leiden's nemesis

- **The Lady Commander/Lucifer** – call-sign **Lucifer**, the Devil of Anger; the commander of the Vogt's elite forces; known as an Immaculate from the Marcs family and a Vogt military officer but not as a koganzug user or Devil

- **Zeb** – from the call-sign Beelzebub, the Devil of Gluttony; a poison expert

Technology

- **Koganzug (kog-an-zoog)** - a combat armor system surgically installed into the user's body; the armor issues biomechs through nodes; the biomechs cover the entire body and can be manipulated by the user's kognitive auxiliary AI; a koganzug creates a network of biomechs that connect to and piggyback on a user's anatomical systems, allowing the user to integrate their koganzug with their bodily functions and senses

- **Biomechs** – nano machines surgically infused into a koganzug user's body; they can be stored and repaired in the nodes; they are powered by kinetic energy and the user's caloric energy

- **Kog Port** - a port surgically installed where the

back of the neck meets the head; it allows a koganzug user to receive software updates and biomech transfusions; it also gives Kog Prime access to the user's neural network to perform neural restorations

- **Kog Prime** – an artificial intelligence that manages all koganzug users (not only the Devils) and operates the Kognitive Network; supposedly it is subject to the Vogt Chairman; it has the ability to "reclaim" koganzug users

- **Kognitive Network** – the technology, data, and communications transmitted between koganzug users, konsole systems, kognitive auxiliaries, and Kog Prime

- **Kognitive Auxiliary** – a limited artificial intelligence that manages a koganzug user's biomechs and local data archive and acts as a software host when Kog Prime connects with a koganzug user; an auxiliary speaks directly into a user's cochlear nerve and can read the muscle movements of the user's lips and tongue to communicate; an auxiliary records everything a user sees and hears analyze the data for more details and can manipulate the user's senses, such as improving their hearing or altering their sight, upon their user's command; kognitive auxiliaries are programmed as rudimentary copies of Kog Prime; when Kog Prime syncs with a kognitive auxiliary it receives accesses to all of the auxiliary's recordings; this process is also supposed to homogenize an auxiliary's personality, removing any variant code that developed while the auxiliary was isolated from Kog Prime

- **Dark Mode** – a state of signal isolation a koganzug user can implement with a password from their superior officer (or Kog Prime); using Dark Mode cuts off communication from Kog Prime and prevents the user from giving off a biomech "surge" that would alert other koganzug users to their presence

- **Neural Restoration** – a form of disciplinary action and mental manipulation Kog Prime uses on koganzug users; the process destroys neural networks in the user's brain, impacting their memories and supposedly setting them back to a specific point in time, called a restore point

- **Reclamation** - a process that Kog Prime is able to use that remotely brain damages a koganzug user, leaving them in a primitive and feral state

- **Korrectives** – a medicine widely used to combat biological sensitivity to the environment, a sensitivity that can result in contracting Blood Rot; some individuals, such as Immaculates, have much stronger sensitivity than others; hollowberns do not need korrectives; Leiden needs to take korrectives regularly because of his body's strong sensitivity to his koganzug hardware when his koganzug is not deployed

- **Plague Blades** – relics dating back to the Origins War that re-engineers have not been able to replicate; they come in a variety of weapon forms; the wounds these weapons make contract Blood Rot; these blades easily penetrate koganzug armor

- **Anzug (An-zoog)** – a suit of armor that must be donned; commonly used by foot soldiers and mercenaries; it can enhance strength and speed and provide camouflage

- **Re-engineering/Re-engineers** – archaeologists excavate relics and stored data from sites around the world and re-engineers endeavor to replicate the relic technology and materials

- **Relics** – objects dating back to the Origins War or earlier; excavated from archaeological sites around the world or handed down in families as heirlooms

Organizations

- **Vogt (Fogt) Faction** – a branch of the Coalition government that rebelled, igniting the Reichland civil war; after Bergverk, it took over the Reichland and was renamed "Das Vogt der Wahrheit," The Steward of Truth Government

- **Devils** – a group of elite koganzug users that work for the Vogt military as assassins, spies, and enforcers; they each have a Devil's mask that acts as an identity and status marker; they are idolized by citizens of the Vogt; they are not allowed to reveal their personal information, like their true faces or names, to anyone, including their comrades

- **Children of Zaybel** – a resistance group that actively attacks and sabotages projects run by or related to the Vogt; responsible for the acrobat terrorist attack at the Peace Banquet and possibly the train bombing in the Dustlands

- **The Merchant Guild Coalition Government** – referred to as the Coalition Government, this group used trade and trade routes to control the Reichland for several decades until the Vogt Faction rebelled and ultimately overthrew them

Religions

- **Arkism** – the most prominent religion on the planet; worships Immaculates and their ancestors, the "Lights Above" and the "Gods Below"; dates back to the Origins War

- **Neo-Arkists** – a religious movement within the Arkist Church that focuses on blood status and reproduction; they instigated and carried out the Hollowbern purge in the Reichland, claiming that hollowberns must be cleansed because they are cursed with sterility; their symbol is an old man holding a giant key

- **Arkist churches** – most towns in the Reichland have an Arkist Church that acts as a center of activity; outside of the Reichland, many places built Arkist Churches manned by Arkist missionaries to entice investment and trade by Arkists

- **Arkist Sanctuaries** – Arkist holy sites where Immaculates and disciples can go for rest and recuperation; these sites have immense archaeological value and much of the church's power is derived from managing these sites

- **Noah** – the title of the leader of the Arkist Church

- **Helmsman** – the title of the leader of an individual Arkist congregation

- **The Twelve Noahs** – according to Arkist history, the Twelve Noahs were the first Immaculates to emerge from the "Lights Above" and wrote The Major Annals and created the Manual language

- **Arkist Missionaries** – agents sent out by the Arkist Church to proselyte and to act as intermediaries for the Arkist Church to new regions and people; after forming an alliance, the Vogt used this network to spread its influence into other countries

Social Classes

- **Blood Status** – the cast system on this world is based on how human a person looks, or the "purity" of their blood/bloodline and how it relates to the First Immaculates

- **First Immaculates** – the first people recorded in history to appear entirely human; all of these individuals date back to the Origins War and are the progenitors of the Immaculate Great Houses

- **Immaculate Registry** – a literal registry where the names of Immaculates around the world are recorded along with their pedigrees

- **Immaculate** – a person who is born looking entirely human, meaning they have black, brown, blond, or red hair; skin in shades of brown and free of any large streaks, blotches, or patterns; eyes in colors of blue, gray, green, hazel, brown, or black; no abnormal features such as spines, horns, claws, tympanic membranes, scales, elongated canines, etc…; they are particularly sensitive to blood rot and must take korrectives regularly or live in a controlled environment

- **Lowly** – a person who is born with one or more non-human feature; many Lowlies have surgeries performed in order to look more like an Immaculate; the lowest ranked Lowlies do not have these surgeries or have features that cannot be hidden or changed

- **Slave** – a person dependent on a contracted alliance with someone of a higher blood status (usually someone from a Great House) to make a living; most of the lowest ranked Lowlies are slaves

- **Hollowbern** – someone born with blood rot stains that do not harm their health; they appear totally Immaculate except for the blood rot stains; they are born sterile; many people believe the stains are contagious (they are not) or hollowberns bring bad luck

- **Fallen** – unregistered Immaculates that have either failed to or refused to be adopted into a Great House or have been disowned by their Great House; they are usually hunted down and assassinated by the Great Houses or the Arkist Church but are sometimes turned into slaves; Fallen slaves have the broken wings tattoo on their backs

- **Great Houses** – the network of Immaculates, Lowlies, and slaves associated with a specific Immaculate family name; the Great Houses are managed by the direct lineage family members of that name

Languages

- **Manual** –an ancient language used to write The Annals; spoken in the Reichland for public speaking and academics; revered in the Arkist Church as the language of the Twelve Noahs

- **Narrisch (Nar-rish)** – a dialect of Manual spoken most commonly in the North and East regions of the Reichland

- **Common** – the most widely spoken language on the planet; Common is a slang language derived from the dead languages recorded in The Minor Annals; if it is not a person's first language, it is often their second

- **The Major Annals** – a compilation of ancient records that predate the Origins War; they recount history, legends, and other stories not from this planet and present science and technology—some of which has not been proved yet; all of these records were written in Manual and excavated from Arkist sanctuaries

- **The Minor Annals** – a compilation of ancient records predating the Origins War; they recount history, legends, and other stories not from this planet and in languages other than Manual; most of this compilation is books, both fiction and non-fiction; these records were excavated from Arkist sanctuaries

- **The Lesser Stories** – any ancient records predating the Origins War excavated from archaeological sites other than the Arkist sanctuaries; many of these records have not been translated because their languages have been lost

Places

- **The Reichland** – the homeland of the Arkist Church; vast forests in the south, fertile plains in the center, and mineral rich steppes in the northeast

- **Giya (Ghee-yuh)** – the country "cupped" by the Reichland east of the Kaltstein Mountains; a desert, the Dustlands, spans the center of the country until reaching the Rettung coastal valley and gulf on the Amiran Strait

- **Dustlands** – an immense desert in Giya where

Leiden lived with his family as a child

- **Bergverk** – a mining town built into a mountain in the Reichland; the last stronghold of the Coalition Government; massacred and razed by the Vogt to end the civil war

- **Port of Rettung** – the largest port in the world located on the southern coast of Giya in the Rettung coastal valley and gulf off of the Amiran Strait; Rettung is subject to massive tides due to the orbit of the Sister Moon

- **Baumfeld (Bom-feld)** – a town in the Dustlands where Leiden lived with his family as a child; specialized in growing strauch trees

- **Traege (Tray-guh) River** – a major river in Giya that has fresh water near the mountains but picks up salt in the Dustlands and becomes undrinkable

- **The Salt Sanctuary** – the Arkist sanctuary in Giya

Plants and Animals

- **Strauch (strouk) tree** – one of the few plants that grow in the Dustlands; the Dustlands' main exports are strauch bark for smoking or chewing and strauch tree incense; the plant is low-growing and scraggly with short needles and grows waxy purple berries used to make incense; the bark can be smoked or chewed

- **Microraptor** – a small, reptilian bird with feathered

wings, needle-like teeth, and clawed appendages on their wings; there are a variety of species; omnivorous scavengers and predators

- **Urvogel (er-foh-gull)** – a large microraptor species often domesticated for meat and eggs by Dustlanders; scavenger and predator

- **Cynodont (s/ái/-noh-dont)** – a mammal-like reptile with a large head and heavy shoulders; grows to be the size of a child; different species display different traits; meat-eating scavenger

- **Compso** – short for compsognathus; a small, bipedal reptile with a long neck, narrow beak, and long, whip-like tail; scavenger and predator

- **Spined rat** – a small, lizard-like mammal with keratinized spikes along its back; omnivorous scavenger

- **Bellydragger** – a nickname in the Dustlands for a predator that carries itself low to the ground

- **Skink** – a group of lizards identified by their snake-like bodies and short legs; species vary in sizes and number of legs; usually eats insects

- **Natter** – a snake-like reptile; eats insects and small animals

Miscellaneous

- **The Annals** – the term "The Annals" refers to the

Glossary

Major Annals and the Minor Annals

- **Black Dust** – an anomaly; this dust comes from dead golems and people who die of blood rot; it can be turned into other materials and is the sole means for re-engineers to imitate materials made by unknown processes; koganzug users use it to create biomechs; makerbugs eat it

- **Golems** – mysterious creatures that appear randomly in nature and have unique physical traits and high intelligence; they breed with a local species, creating non-golem hybrids; golems turn into Black Dust when they die

- **Makerbugs** – insect-like creatures that can fly and live in large colonies called hives; their stings inject blood rot into their victims, which turn into Black Dust as they die, and they eat the Black Dust; biomechs are made using makerbugs

- **Letters** – Leiden agrees to deliver Wilhelm's letter to his daughter in Rettung, hoping she will help him remove his koganzug; Wilhelm's daughter wrote a letter to her father that Leiden reads often, the epitaphs in this book are quotes from that letter

- **Totems** – Devils have personal items called totems that they use to help them remember their identities after their koganzug installation surgeries or after Kog Prime performs a neural restoration on them

- **Schal (shaal)** – a garment worn by Dustlanders as a coming-of-age symbol that can be wrapped around the head, the shoulders, the neck, or the waist;

usually displays ornate embroidery

- **Blood rot** – a disease contracted from the environment, a plague blade, or a makerbug sting; the victim disintegrates into Black Dust until their organs fail; prevented by korrectives or treated using antiserum; hollowberns cannot contract blood rot; widespread superstition that victims are contagious and attract misfortune

- **Dunkelheit (Doon-kel-h/ái/t) Festival** – a week-long festival that takes place in Giya when the Sister Moon sets late in the year; marks the end of Growing Season and the beginning of Fallow Season in the Dustlands and the Low Tide on the coast

- **Mondlikt Festival** – a week-long festival that takes place in Giya when the Sister Moon rises; marks the end of the fallow season and the beginning of the growing season in the Dustlands and the beginning of high tide on the coast

Acknowledgements

A huge thank you to my husband Matt for his encouragement and support. I'm not me without him so this book wouldn't be either.

Also, a huge thank you to KC Hunting for the many late nights of brainstorming and commiserating—without them, I would be even less sane than I am now.

Thank you to my Writers of the Future Cohort—writing is hard; misery loves company—and thank you to my beta readers KC Hunting, Erin Cairns, Jon Ficke, my parents, and my Writing Group peers Jeffrey Creer, Darci Rhoades Stone, Carl Duzett, Piper Vasicek, and Joe Vasicek. It is rough work reading a rough draft; your feedback was poorly received but well applied. Please excuse the occasional tantrums.

A special thank you to my mom Linda Henrie for being my proofreader; my dad Tony Henrie for being my copy editor; and, my other family members for reading various terrible drafts of this novel over the years. Your help saved me money and time, and your support and enthusiasm saved my writing career.

A huge thank you to Duncan Halleck for letting me use the illustration he created for the short story "All Light and Darkness" found in L. Ron Hubbard Present Writers of the Future Volume 34 as my cover art. May he be forever blessed for his talent and kindness!

Lastly, thank you to Dave Wolverton (1957-2022).

His recognition and appreciation for my writing was a huge part of why I continued to pursue this project despite the chaos and time it has demanded. May he rest in peace and his words endure.

Many have supported me during the six years it has taken me to write this first novel. Thank you for your help, interest, and enthusiasm. My passion keeps me writing, but your encouragement keeps me willing to share it.

About the Author

Amy Henrie Gillett lives in Utah where she enjoys hiking, fishing, and not skiing. She oversees a household consisting of her partner in crime, three young ninjas destined for grand adventures and many groundings, a dog with questionable intelligence, a delusional white cat, a few spoiled fish (figuratively, not literally), as well as a few pet snails and a gecko who dreams of eating them.

Needless to say, if Amy is not writing, gardening, or watching Asian dramas, she is taking care of one of the above.

To find out more, check out her website: amyhenriegillett.com.